BLACK
BARK

Black
Bark

by

Brian Evenson

Black Shuck Books
www.BlackShuckBooks.co.uk

Versions of the following stories first appeared as follows:
'Black Bark' in *A Collapse of Horses* (Coffee House Press, 2016)
'The Cabin' in *Come Join Us by the Fire* 2 (Nightfire, 2020)
'Grottor' and 'The Dismal Mirror' in *Windeye* (Coffee House Press, 2012)
'Contagion' in *Contagion* (Wordcraft, 2000; reprinted by Astrophil Press, 2016)

Cover design & internal layout © WHITEspace 2023
www.white-space.uk

First published in the UK by Black Shuck Books, 2023

978-1-913038-94-6

—for Laird Hunt

They'd been riding two days straight now, climbing farther and farther up into the mountains in a bitter wind, searching for the cabin Sugg claimed was supposed to be there. Things had not gone smooth. Sugg had taken one in the leg, the thigh, and the blood had dripped down inside his pant leg and into his boot. Now, Rawley saw, the boot was overfull, and Sugg was leaving a drizzle of blood along the trail behind them. The side of Sugg's stolen tovero too was slicked with it, and the slick had taken on a vaguely human shape, as if Sugg's leg jostling back and forth against the horse had been trying to draw someone with his blood.

"We got to stop," said Rawley. "You need to rest."

For a long time Sugg didn't answer. Then he said, in a voice just above a whisper, "It's around here somewhere. Bound to come across it any moment."

"Where?" asked Rawley. There'd been nothing for miles. When Sugg didn't answer, he said, "It's going to be dark soon."

But Sugg just kept on. Or didn't rein his horse in, anyway. Maybe the horse was just following its own path.

They were following a trail that flirted with the fast-moving creek, curving toward it and then away again. At first Sugg hadn't been sure it was the right creek. Now he claimed to be sure, but Rawley guessed he didn't know for certain. He'd been saying for hours the cabin was just around the next curve, around the next bend, but no cabin ever was.

~

"Going to be dark soon," Rawley repeated. "We should stop, make camp."

Again it took a long time for Sugg to answer, but when he did, his voice sounded a little stronger. "They still following?" he asked.

Rawley shook his head, spat. "Haven't been for hours," he said. "We shook them."

"Maybe they just want us thinking so," said Sugg. "Maybe they're trying to take us off guard."

Rawley shook his head again. "Naw," he said. "It's just us."

Sugg was swaying a little in the saddle. For a moment Rawley eased back on his reins and watched him.

"Sugg," he said. "Sugg, you got to stop."

Sugg didn't say anything, just kept riding.

"Sugg," Rawley called after him. "I'm stopping here. I mean it."

But Sugg didn't look back. He just kept going, still swaying, keeping to his slow, leisurely pace as it took him around a bend in the path and he disappeared from Rawley's view.

Cursing under his breath, Rawley spurred his horse and followed.

~

He hadn't been far behind, but when Rawley came around the bend, Sugg and the tovero were nowhere. He reined up and took a closer look at the tovero's track, but it just ended, abruptly. He backtracked and looked for a break off the trail they might have taken, but there was nothing he could see. He cursed, louder this time.

"Sugg!" he shouted, and when there was no answer, he took out his pistol and shot it once in the air. He waited the echo out, then listened, but didn't hear any response. He nudged his own stolen horse along with his spurs until it was loping. He followed the trail around the next bend, but Sugg wasn't there either.

~

He followed the trail up a half mile or so, looking for some sign of Sugg's cabin, but there was still no sign of habitation anywhere. As he climbed, the leaves of the aspens were suddenly already yellowing. The path bucked closer to the creek, and the water's rumble grew louder. He watched the sunlight slide up the side of the slope and disappear, leaving the air suddenly chill, the papery bark of the trees slowly graying in the fading light.

Across the river, he spotted the mouth of a cave; or maybe it was an old mineshaft. He found a place to ford and splashed his horse across. On the other side he dismounted, tied the reins to a tree, and climbed the bare shale slope, slipping, up to the entrance.

Not a mineshaft. Just an ordinary cave. It was dry inside, with a fairly level floor, and smelled of dust. He couldn't tell how far back it went. Somebody had arranged a circle of worn, ash-smeared stones near one of the walls. A fire pit. Not a cabin, but it was shelter. It'd do.

He started down to gather some wood. There were enough dead and dry branches scattered around that it took just a minute or two to gather a decent stack. Though the sun had slid behind the peak, there was still light left. He tried to gauge how long it would last, but found it impossible to tell without the sun. Could last another five minutes or another twenty. No moon yet, but he didn't know if that meant it was yet to appear or it wasn't coming. He sighed and dropped the branches near his horse, then untied the reins and went back to see if he couldn't find Sugg after all.

He spurred the horse at first and then just settled back to let it take its own way. It galloped for a bit, then loped, then slowed until he spurred it again, rubbing his hand along its neck as he did so, trying to stay friends. Five minutes of decent riding and the light had all but dwindled. A minute later and he could hardly see.

He was readying to rein up and return to the cave when he saw a dim shape athwart the trail. He went close and squinted, finally got down, and bent over it. Only by touching it did he become sure it was a man.

"Sugg?" he said. "Where's your horse?"

"Gone," said Sugg. The man was limp, hardly moving, and he smelled of oil and blood.

"You all right?" asked Rawley.

Sugg just gave a low chuckle.

"Come on," said Rawley. "Found a cave."

When Sugg didn't say anything, Rawley hauled him to his feet. Sugg couldn't stand, couldn't keep his feet under him, so in the end Rawley had to drop him. It took a few more tries before he had the man up and across his back and was staggering under his weight. A few good heaves and Sugg was slung over the saddle of the horse, who made it clear it didn't want no part of it. But finally it was done. Taking the horse by the reins, Rawley headed for the cave.

~

In the dark he missed it at first and had to double back. No moon had come up, none at all. In the end he only found the cave again because he remembered the way the creek had sounded right near it, but it took stopping and setting fire to a dead branch to find where to cross the river, and even then some searching still to make out the cave's mouth.

He put the horse down below to graze, left the torch to burn itself out on the shale, and slung Sugg over his shoulder. Sugg groaned once but otherwise didn't hardly move. Rawley stumbled his way up the shale with him, slipping and falling and once even dropping the man, but finally he pushed the fellow up over the lip and into the cave's mouth. He went back down for the tinder and his bedroll before clambering in for good himself.

"This the cabin?" asked Sugg from the floor, his voice barely above a whisper.

"No," said Rawley. "But it's shelter."

"Not far now," said Sugg absently. "Just around the next bend."

Rawley ignored him.

~

He seated Sugg against the wall while he arranged the branches, got a fire going. He kept it low, both in case they were still following and because he didn't want to fill the cave with smoke, but there was still some warmth to it if you were close. It wasn't no cabin, but it wasn't open country either. It would do.

In the flickering light, Sugg looked pale, almost dead. Rawley said his name once and then repeated it. Sugg did not seem to hear.

Rawley circled his way around the fire and shook him.

"Here," whispered Sugg. "Still here."

Rawley carefully worked off the other man's boot. He kept expecting Sugg to moan or flinch but he never did, neither spoke nor moved. When the boot finally came loose, it came with a rush of blood, spattering Rawley's hands and his own boots. *How much blood can the man have left in him?* Rawley wondered.

He slit open Sugg's soaked pant leg with his knife, then carefully peeled back the dressing. The skin beneath, once he sopped up the blood, appeared livid, the lips of the wound puckered and swollen. He cleaned it best he could, then bound it up again in the same sodden dressing. Then he circled back to his own side of the fire and sat.

"You're still alive, right?" Rawley asked. When Sugg didn't answer, he came back around the fire pit and prodded Sugg's side with his boot, repeating the question.

"What?" asked Sugg. When he spoke, he didn't move his lips hardly at all, it seemed to Rawley. Or maybe he did. Maybe it was just the flames and shadow that made it seem so.

Rawley leaned over, spat. It didn't hit the fire but sizzled on one of the rocks forming the edge of the fire pit. "You're still alive?" asked Rawley for the third time.

"What kind of question is that?"

"You're going to lose the leg," said Rawley.

There was silence for a long while, then a strange high-pitched wheezing that it took Rawley a moment to realize was Sugg laughing.

~

Rawley sat still, staring into the fire. He was hungry, but it still felt good to be off a horse.

"Got food in the cabin?" he asked.

"Sure," said Sugg. "Help yourself."

Rawley kept staring. There was something about the way the air drew in the cave that made the fire go from leaping high to nearly guttering, all in the course of a few seconds. He couldn't stop staring.

He breathed in deep. "Tomorrow," he said. "Tomorrow, you stay here. I'll go see if I can find the cabin."

"Tomorrow I'll be just where I am," said Sugg.

"What do you mean?" asked Rawley, confused, but Sugg didn't answer. "That's a strange way to put it," said Rawley. "When are you not just where you are?"

"Exactly," said Sugg.

Rawley stared farther into the fire, deeper this time. When he came to himself, he was not sure how much time had passed. He shook his head back and forth to clear it. "We should get some sleep," he said. He turned and started to stretch out on the cave floor, jostling about to get comfortable. He was almost there when, so softly he wasn't sure at first that he'd heard it, Sugg called his name.

"What is it, Sugg?" he asked.

"Something in my boot I need," said Sugg. "Reach down and pull it out for me?"

"The boot you're wearing or the boot you're not?"

"Not," Sugg said.

"The bloody one," said Rawley, flatly.

"The bloody one," confirmed Sugg.

"Like hell I'm reaching into that blood-soaked thing," Rawley said. He pulled himself up onto his elbows. Across the fire, Sugg still hadn't moved. "It's not sanitary. What you after, anyway?"

When there was no answer, Rawley sighed. He pulled himself over and reached, fumbled the boot up off the stone floor, then rolled until he was sitting up. He upended it, shook it, but nothing came out. He knocked its heel against the floor a few times, then upended it again. Still nothing. He tossed it back. It lay flopped over Sugg's foot.

"What you say it was?" asked Rawley.

"Didn't say," said Sugg. "A good-luck charm."

"No, there's nothing there," said Rawley.

"Figures," said Sugg.

They stayed there watching the fire quiver. It was, Rawley thought, like a living, breathing

thing. As soon as he thought that, the fire grew dim, threatened to go out.

"We should stretch out and get some sleep," Rawley said.

"I'm fine," Sugg's voice said over the glow of the coals. "You stretch out. I'm just fine here."

"All right," said Rawley. But for some reason he kept sitting there, staring into the fire and at the dark shape of Sugg across from him.

~

He didn't know how much time had passed. Maybe a long time, maybe just a little. It was as if the dying fire had hypnotized him, or maybe he'd fallen asleep. But when suddenly he heard Sugg's voice, he wasn't sure if he was dreaming or if Sugg was really talking.

"Know the story of black bark?" Sugg's voice asked. It was completely dark now. Rawley couldn't see even the barest glimpse of the other man. He waved his fingers in front of his face but couldn't see those either.

"Black what?" he asked.

"Bark," said Sugg.

"Like from a tree?"

"Sure," said Sugg. "Why not?"

"What do you mean, why not?" asked Rawley, more awake now, irritated. "Either it is or it isn't."

It was as if Sugg hadn't heard. He was already telling the story. "A man found a piece of black bark in his coat pocket," he said. "He wasn't sure how it had gotten there. It was just there."

He paused for long enough that Rawley asked, "And that's the story?"

"More or less," said Sugg. "The whole of it gathers up in those words, in that beginning. Everything else is just teasing it out."

"What kind of story is that?"

"Shall we tease it out?" asked Sugg.

Rawley shrugged, then realized Sugg wouldn't see it. "Go to sleep," he said.

"You'll sleep soon enough," said Sugg. "For now, listen."

~

"A man found a piece of black bark in his coat pocket," repeated Sugg. "He wasn't sure how it had gotten there. It was just there.

"He took it out and stared at it. He wasn't sure where it came from, what kind of tree, if it was a tree."

"What else has bark?" asked Rawley, feeling suddenly very strange.

"This man too was the sort of man who only knew about the bark of trees," said Sugg. "Like you. And in his mind, he went through all the trees he knew but couldn't think of any with bark as black as this. Maybe that should have told him something. But he just looked at the piece of black bark for a long while and then tossed it away.

"The next time he put on his coat, there it was again."

"What do you mean, there it was again?" asked Rawley, his voice rising.

"Just what I said. There it was again."

"But he threw it away."

"Yes," said Sugg. "He did."

"Then how did it get back in his pocket?"

"That's not part of the story," said Sugg. "That's the part that gets left out. I'm telling black bark, and I know what's part of it and what isn't. Hush and listen.

"The next time he put on his coat, there it was again. He took that piece of black bark out, threw it down, then reached in his pocket, and it was there again, back in the same pocket. He took it out and threw it into the fire, and a moment later, there it was back in his pocket."

"Why would you tell me this?" asked Rawley.

"No matter where he threw it, it came back to him. He thought he was going mad. Finally he took the black bark out of his pocket, set it on the table, and picked up a hammer. But when he went to hit it with the hammer, it opened its eye and looked at him."

"Its what?" Rawley interrupted.

"Its eye," said Sugg.

"Eye?" said Rawley. "But bark don't—"

"Don't interrupt," said Sugg's voice. "Its eye. Yes, that's what I said. Eye. And don't you try to puzzle it out none and think that it means something other than what I said. Every time you think you have the world figured, trust me, that's just when the world's got you figured and is about to spring and break your back.

"When he went to hit it with the hammer, the black bark opened its eye and looked at him. That was all, just looked. But for a long time, and without blinking. The man looked too, and though he wanted to, found he couldn't look away. Then the black bark closed its eye, and he could look away. So the man lifted it up careful as he could, put it in his pocket, and left it there until he was dead. Once he was dead, it didn't have no use for him."

~

When he woke up, the morning was well on. His eyelashes had gotten gummed together during the night somehow, and he had to rub them before they'd open enough for him to see clearly. Sugg was gone, though how that could be Rawley had no clue – the man had hardly been able to move, let alone walk. Where he'd been propped up the night before, the cave wall was covered in a swath of blood rendered in a vaguely human shape. Like the shape on Sugg's horse. Hard to believe Sugg still had that much blood in him, considering what he must already have lost. So much blood, and in the shape of a man. *Blood angel*, thought Rawley, then he shook his head, trying to push the words out of his mind.

He stood and rolled up his bedroll, then paused at the mouth of the cave, trying to get as much of a view of the land behind him as possible. No sign of pursuit that he could see. No sign of Sugg either.

He picked his way down to the creek, washed the blood off his face and hands, drank deep. His horse was there, peaceful, the vegetation around it cropped close. He saddled it, rode.

He kept on up the same trail, not knowing what else to do. Maybe the cabin was up ahead somewhere, or some cabin, anyway. He rode through groves of quaking aspen shot through with fingers of juniper pine. The peaks ahead were spattered with snow in places, bare granite where exposed. It was very cold. Why would anybody have a cabin here?

He found a scrubby crab-apple tree and gnawed on a few of the hard fruits just to get something besides water in his stomach. The skin of them made his lips itch. There was still no cabin, nor any sign of one. When a path split off from the trail, he followed it to a boarded-over mine entrance.

By noon, he'd begun to grow dizzy. He found what he thought was some yellow dock, seeds brown and starting to drop. He ate handfuls of them, broke the plant at the stem and stripped back the skin to get at the pith, then sat in the shade until he felt well enough to keep going.

After a while his stomach started to cramp up, his skin grown clammy. He kept riding but slower now, hunched over. A few times he stopped and kneeled at the side of the trail, heaving, but nothing came out.

He drank some water and convinced himself he felt at least a little better, but there were still patches of time when he wasn't sure what or who he was, when he would come to himself on a stretch of trail with no idea how he'd gotten there.

By early afternoon, the trail had begun to peter out, and he had a hard time following it. Soon after, he lost it altogether.

~

It was near dusk by the time he made it back down to the cave. He was tempted to keep going, down and past it, but he was exhausted, his horse too. No, better to stop a few hours in a place he knew, wait a little, rest a little, continue back down in the morning.

Near the cave, beside the creek, he found Sugg's horse. The blood angel was still swathed on its side, nearly black now in the failing light. "Sugg?" he called in a cracked voice, but nobody answered. Sugg hadn't had the horse yesterday when Rawley found him. It must have just wandered up here on its own, caught the scent of Rawley's own horse, maybe, or of Sugg himself. The horse didn't mean anything.

Still, despite that, when he climbed up the shale slope, he was relieved to find the cave was empty.

~

He lay on the floor of the cave in the dark, shivering. *Get up*, he kept telling himself, *start a fire*. But he just kept lying there.

Outside he heard the horses neighing. He expected them to settle quickly, but they didn't – something continued to agitate them. He closed his hand over the grip of his revolver. If he had to, he told himself, he could go out there and take care of it.

It grew dark, then darker still. It was so dark he wasn't sure where the cave's opening was anymore. Everything seemed the same dark around him. Even if he wanted to gather firewood, he wouldn't know where to go.

After a while, he started feeling warmer, and drowsy. He didn't need a fire, he told himself. All he needed was a little sleep. Tomorrow he'd start out fresh, ride back down the mountain, find food, find shelter, start life over again.

~

He woke to the warm glow of a fire. He lay there, staring into it, watching the flames weave back and forth. When he looked up, there was Sugg standing over him. He was swaying slightly, one boot missing, his clothing stiff with blood.

"Where the hell you come from?" Rawley asked. Or thought he asked. He wasn't sure if his lips moved. He tried to sit up but found he couldn't move. Sugg stayed looming over him a moment and then shuffled over to the other side of the fire, sitting heavily in the same spot he had been the night before, the spot marked out for him by his blood.

Sugg reached his hand into the fire and stirred it around. Sparks flew up, and the air smelled for an instant of burned hair. The flames didn't seem to bother Sugg, and he pulled his hand only slowly free.

"Comfy?" asked Sugg. "Still alive?"

Inside his head, Rawley asked, *What's happening? What's wrong with me?* Outside, the head didn't move.

"Doesn't matter much one way or the other," said Sugg. Then he opened his mouth wide and smiled. It was a terrible thing to watch. Rawley began to be very afraid.

For a long time Sugg just stayed there smiling. Then, just as suddenly, his face relaxed. "Shall I tell you a story?" he asked.

No, thought Rawley.

"Shall I tell you the story of not black bark?" he asked. "The story of everything black bark left out?"

No, thought Rawley. *Please.*

"A story, then," said Sugg. "A last one for the road. I'll make it a good one." He smiled again, that same terrible smile. Then his lips formed the words, "Let's begin."

I.

His name was Beckwourth, but he usually went by just Beck, and up mountain he mostly didn't have to go by anything at all. With nobody around, a name wasn't hardly needed except to keep yourself sane. Sometimes when he made it down far enough to trade and someone reached out their hand to introduce themselves, he had to stop and think before his name came back to him.

That morning he left camp well before light. Smelling the promise of snow on the air the night before, he hoped to check his traps before winter set in. But when he parted his shelter's canvas flap, he saw snow already coming down.

He tramped through it and down to the edge of the lake, rifle strapped to his back. Quickly he found the stake attached to the chain of the first trap. The trap had been sprung, the bait taken, but nothing was caught. He baited and reset it, careful of its teeth, and trudged off toward the next one.

The air was cold, his breath icing into frost on his beard. Snow gathered on his arms and shoulders; from time to time he shook it off. The crunch of his footsteps in the snow was sharp and loud, the frozen air making them sound like they were coming from someplace else.

The second trap had been sprung too and, when he reached it, the third as well, nothing in either. The snow was falling thicker, the sun a hazy enucleated eye. Judging by its position, he was running slow. He would have to be careful if he were to make it back before dark.

The fourth trap wasn't there at all. The stake had been torn completely out of the ground. The bushes nearby were broken and displaced by whatever had rushed through them. He started to track the creature's path, but quickly lost it in the snow.

He stopped and considered. He could continue around the edge of the lake to the other traps or he could turn back. But turning back would take nearly as long as continuing around. Either way, he wasn't likely to make it back before dark.

He did not know which path to choose.

Maybe there's another path, something in him whispered. The surface of the lake was frozen hard, safe enough to cross. Couldn't he check one more trap and then, instead of either circling back or continuing on around, simply walk straight across the lake?

The fifth trap was just as empty as the other three, though this time at least the trap itself was still there. Was there time to check the sixth? No, he didn't think so. Not safely. Better to set off across the lake and hope to reach camp before dark.

He stepped down onto the ice. A few steps in and the ice shuddered then made a sound like a bone breaking. He ignored this. It was cold enough, he knew. The ice would hold.

And yet as he neared what he judged to be the lake's center, the snow atop the ice became slushy. Perhaps it had been melted by the sun, he thought, but then thought no: there had been no direct sun. He tried not to worry. Soon, he was wading through water past his calves. A warm current, maybe? A hidden spring?

He could sense the ice still solid underneath. The slush didn't make any sense: it should all be frozen. He kept going, more tentative now.

When the slush finally lapped at the top of his boots he stopped. He hesitated a moment then turned, sloshing back the way he had come. He would have to go around after all.

~

The snowfall grew heavier. His tracks had leveled and filled and disappeared: there was nothing for him to follow back. No matter, he told himself: soon the slush would end and his tracks would be visible again, even though choked by snow. He just had to walk out of the slush.

But the slush didn't end. He became sure he had walked longer trying to get back than he had going out. Perhaps he had been moving around in circles. He was briefly tempted to veer in a new direction, but knew it would only get him lost.

And then, abruptly, the slush became snow. The snow was falling heavily enough he couldn't see much. He saw no sign of his footsteps, but he kept walking.

He laughed with a kind of wonder when at last he reached the shore. Eagerly he pulled himself through the snowy bushes and back onto land. He expected it to feel different than the lake, but, covered with snow, it hardly did.

A moment later, he stepped into the trap.

II.

He fell when the trap snapped around his leg. For a moment the pain was almost too great to bear and then, slowly, it resolved into a deep throb. Somehow, grunting against the stabs of pain, he managed to turn over and stand again, with all his weight on the other leg, the one not in the trap. Crouching, he wedged his gloved fingers in, trying not to tear the leather on the trap's teeth. Breathing through his own teeth, he struggled to force the trap's jaws apart. Once they began to open, he felt the teeth pulling out of his flesh. The pain rushed back again and he had to consciously resist letting go. Finally he managed, hands shaking, grunting, to withdraw his foot. He held the jaws spread open a few seconds and then released both halves at once. They snapped heavily shut.

He fell back on the snow and lay there, panting, staring at the darkening sky. After a while he managed to sit. Stripping off his gloves, he felt down the side of his boot to the row of punctures. On one side the trap had torn the hide but hadn't gone all the way through to his skin. On the other, blood oozed out of the holes.

He flexed his ankle a little and pain shot through the leg, a little more blood oozing out. Stripping off the other glove he wriggled both hands into the boot, separating the hide from the skin, and slowly working the boot off.

There were deep gashes on the leg, and a darkening band of flesh. He wiggled his toes and they moved; the leg wasn't broken, then. That was something anyway.

He examined the trap. It was one of his: the missing one, its chain still attached to a piece of stake. How had the trap remained set? He had originally assumed an animal, a large one, had stepped into it and dragged it away, but if that were the case, it would have been sprung.

Perhaps someone deliberately moved it?

Who? he thought. *I'm the only one up here.*

~

His foot was growing cold, the band on his leg still darkening. He started to work the boot back on, but he couldn't: the leg was too swollen now to fit.

He slit the boot up along the side, then cut the fringe off one arm of his coat, tying it into two long strands and using these to bind the boot tight around his leg. He managed to get to his feet. None of the nearby bushes had branches large enough for him to use as a crutch. Though his rifle wasn't the right length and the barrel kept jabbing into his side, he could steady himself with it and limp slowly along, wincing. It would do.

He set off. Immediately his slit boot was soaked through, the foot very cold. He was, he knew, likely to lose the foot, some of the leg too. There was no helping it. He stumbled his way along best he could into the darkness.

Would he know when he had circled the lake far enough to reach his camp? Would he, in the darkness, recognize when to strike toward it? Or would he just keep circling the lake, hour after hour, until he was dead?

~

Soon he could no longer feel the leg – which made, he supposed, walking a little easier. He fell twice, but each time managed after a brief rest to pull himself up again. *It is foolish to go on*, a part of his mind whispered. And yet he continued walking. What other choice did he have?

Stop and light a fire, another part of him thought. *Warm up a little, survive until morning.*

A fire, he thought, and his gloves began fumbling at the buttons of his coat so as to get at his matches.

And then suddenly, almost as if by thinking of fire he had made it appear, he saw the light.

It was impossible. It had been weeks since he had seen anyone this high up mountain and nobody was going to suddenly arrive now, with winter setting in. No, it wasn't a light, there was no way it was a light: it was a trick of the darkness, a trick of his mind. It would be wiser to ignore it and start his own fire.

He made his way toward it.

~

The light came from a cabin, but this too was impossible: there were no cabins this high. It streamed out of a pair of windows, the glow dancing and shivering on the snow. That too was wrong: even if there were a cabin, it wouldn't have glass in the windows – they were too far from civilization for that. And even if it did, the windows would have been covered this time of year, draped inside with skins and rugs in an effort to keep the cold out and the heat in.

He knocked. There was no answer. He knocked a second time, and waited. Still no reply. He tried the handle; it was locked.

Stepping away from the door, he peered into the closest window. The glass was frosted over, distorting everything inside. He could make out the glow of the fire and an indistinct figure passing to and fro before it. He wiped at the glass with his hand, scratched at the ice. When the glass remained blurred, he realized there must be a layer of ice on the inside as well.

He rapped on the glass with his glove but it made only a muffled sound. Removing his glove, he rapped again with bare knuckles, the sound sharp now, the report echoing into the night.

The figure inside stopped pacing and stood poised, as if listening, like an animal scenting the air. Beck struck the glass again and then flinched back: a face or something face-like was suddenly pressed to the window: very white, two dark holes for eyes, if they were eyes. Before he could look closer, it was gone.

To one side of him, the door opened. In the light streaming out stood a tall man wearing a dressing gown.

"Yes?" he said. "May I help you?" His manner of speaking struck Beck as unusual – less like English wasn't his native tongue and more as if his mouth objected to the idea of being employed for speech at all. Beck turned too quickly toward him, twisted his hurt leg, and fainted.

III.

He was warm, perhaps too warm. He was inside somewhere, lying on a heap of fur, a fire flickering nearby. A man stood over him, wearing a thin dressing gown made of black silk. He was tall, almost cadaverously thin, his hair going gray at the temples. He peered at Beck intensely.

"He awaketh," the man said.

"I..." Beck began, but wasn't quite sure what to say.

The man left the silence to linger, then finally prompted, "You're lucky to be alive."

"Yes," managed Beck. He pulled himself up higher on the heap of fur. The man watched him struggle but made no move to help.

Once comfortable, Beck looked around. He was in the central room of a cabin, the walls so dark they hardly reflected the firelight. He could just make out, at a little distance, an interior door. *The windows and the front door must be behind me*, he thought. Above him, the roof beams and ceiling were stained dark, visible only by implication, a little gleam here and there as subtle as stars.

Looking up made him feel dizzy. He looked quickly down, saw a packed earth floor, walked on often enough to become smooth and catch the gleam of the firelight. The fire was in a chimney made of dark stone against the wall, its sooted interior even darker. Tacked above it was a crude wooden shelf that displayed a series of five roughly ovoid stones, each the size of a baby's head.

"What are those?" he asked the tall man.

"Would you like to see?"

Beck grunted and tried to rise, sank back again. This time the man reached out to him, pulled him up. The man's hand was very cold. His body had no smell to it. Half-supported by him, Beck made his way closer to the shelf.

It was a series of crude heads, carved out of pumice, a face scratched on each, something written on each face. He moved closer to one. *John*, it said on the left cheek. A surname was on the right: *Colter*.

"What are they?" he asked again.

"Those?" said the man. "Oh, the others who found me. This is how I remember them."

Beck opened his mouth to speak, then thought better of it and shut it. But the man seemed to guess what he intended.

"Don't worry, there'll be a stone for you, too," he said.

For a brief moment Beck experienced an almost irresistible urge to flee, and might have had the man not had a tight grip on his arm. All he could do was turn his head away. With his free hand, the man slowly reached out and cupped Beck's face, then turned it back to look at him.

"What's your name?" the tall man asked.

"Beck."

The tall man slowly shook his head. "Your full name," he said.

Beck had to think a little. He knew he had a name, but it was fluttering almost beyond his reach.

"James," he finally managed. "James Beckwourth. What's yours?"

The tall man smiled. When, after a moment it became clear he was not going to respond, Beck said, "Why did you want to know my name?"

"Why, for your stone," said the man. "Why else?"

~

After a while, how long exactly it was impossible for Beck to say, the tall man released his arm and his head and allowed him to look away. Beck collapsed back onto the pile of furs. The man ambled his way to a wingback chair and sat down. He remained there in the glow of the fire, watching.

"Don't mind me," he eventually said. "Go ahead and sleep."

But the way the voice formed those words made Beck feel it might be wiser to stay awake.

They stayed like that, the tall man's hand slowly kneading the arms of the chair. Sometimes, when the fire was particularly quiet, Beck could hear the sounds of the man's fingers rubbing over the brocade.

The man smiled absently, then turned this smile on Beck.

"Not sleepy?" he asked.

Beck shook his head.

"How shall we pass the time then?" the man asked. "A story?"

"All right," said Beck.

He waited for the tall man to begin. But he did not.

"Well?" the tall man finally said.

"Well what?" asked Beck.

"I'm waiting."

"I thought you were going to tell one," said Beck.

"You're the guest," said the tall man. "I wanted to give you a chance."

Beck did not respond. Soon the man made an exasperated noise and unfolded himself from the chair.

"Where are you going?" asked Beck.

"I can't tell a story without an audience," he said.

Aren't I the audience? wondered Beck.

But he was not. Or, rather, not the only audience. With care, the man wrapped his long fingers around one of the stone heads and lifted it down from the shelf, setting it on the floor. He did the same with each of the heads in turn, until they formed a circle on the floor, a circle completed by Beck's own head and body.

The man paced slowly around the circle. Beck tried to stand, but found that he couldn't rise. "Who are you?" he asked, suddenly afraid.

"I am who you expect me to be," the man said, and passed behind Beck's back. Beck tried to turn his head to follow him, found it would not turn.

The man entered his vision again, on the other side now. "Someone else might see me differently," he said. He gestured at the stones in the circle, still walking. "As indeed all your compatriots did."

He vanished again, behind Beck's back. When he reappeared, he began his story. As he spoke, he kept circling, circling.

~

"There was once a man who lost himself in a snowstorm," began the tall man. "He walked in what he though was a place he knew, but walked in such fashion as to slip into another place altogether."

"What do you mean?" asked Beck, growing alarmed.

"Exactly what I say," said the man.

"Tell me another story instead," said Beck.

"I gave you the chance to tell the story," said the tall man. "You could have told it all night if you wanted. You could have told it until morning. But you chose to forfeit that chance. Now it's my turn.

"This man slipped into another place altogether. He was not the first to have done so. Nor would he be the last."

As he spoke, the tall man moved his hands in front of him, as if he were shaping something out of the air.

"Suffice it to say that in slipping through he hurt himself badly. A fall, say. Or a blow to the head. Or a leg injury."

He smiled in a way that showed his teeth.

"In struggling to find shelter he came to a cabin. Only it wasn't a cabin exactly. It might be better described as a lair or a den. But to him it seemed a cabin. He cannot be blamed for this. Having slipped out of the place he knew, he had not yet learned how to see where he now was.

"He knocked on the door that wasn't a door of the cabin that wasn't a cabin and was admitted. The front room of the cabin was empty, though there was a fire burning. *Hello?* the man called, but nobody answered. And so, lonely, hurt, famished, the man imagined someone to be there."

"He what?" said Beck.

"Nothing unusual about that," said the man. "Particularly for someone who has not yet begun to see. And perhaps I misspoke. There *was* someone in the cabin, or rather something, only not in the front room. There was another room, another chamber, another cave, and in it something slept. The thing that slept was dreaming, and it was this dream that this man, let's call him, say, Colter, though almost any name would do, had imagined into a person."

"But how can you—"

"Don't interrupt," said the tall man. "I'm warning you." And he disappeared behind Beck's back again.

"Eventually, though," said the voice from behind him, "he began to see and then, abruptly, the person he imagined was there was there no longer. All that was left was the room he was in, a door in its back wall. This Colter could not help himself. He opened the door.

"The room on the other side was very dark. Even when he opened the door wide it was as if the light from the fire could not enter the room. Colter made the mistake of going in anyway."

Beck strained to get up. He still could not move. "Please," he said. "Don't—"

And then abruptly he found he couldn't speak. The man slowed his restless circling, stopped, and showed Beck what he had been shaping out of the air.

It was a stone head. *James* and been written on one cheek, *Beckwourth* on the other. He had made a crude mouth as well, a row of x's across it, as if the lips had been sewn shut with thread.

"Do you like it?" the tall man asked. And then, "Cat's got your tongue? Just nod or shake your head. I think we can, for the moment, allow that much."

Suddenly Beck could move his head. He shook it desperately. The tall man frowned and began to make the stone head he held nod, and then Beck felt himself nodding too.

"Good," the tall man said, his voice just above a whisper, his eyes little more than slits now. "I'm glad we agree."

He started circling again. He was changing now, thinning out, becoming impossibly tall, becoming less human.

"This Colter went into the darkness. He could see nothing, but he knew something was there: he could hear the sound of it breathing deeply as it slept."

He tipped the stone head sharply back in his hands and Beck felt his own head thrown back, heard a scream issue from his own throat.

"Eventually," said the tall man who was no longer man, "it woke up."

He stepped into the center of the circle and very carefully placed the stone in Beck's lap, then adjusted Beck's hands until they held it. When he stepped back again, Beck could see five men sitting around him, crosslegged, unable to move anything but their eyes, each holding a stone head with a name on it.

"Now you begin to see," murmured the tall man.

Help me, thought Beck. He couldn't help but think everyone in the circle must be thinking the same thing, and had been thinking it for a very long time, all to no avail.

The tall man stared down at him.

"Of course it's just a story," the tall man said, and smiled. "What actually is going to happen, I promise you, is much, much worse."

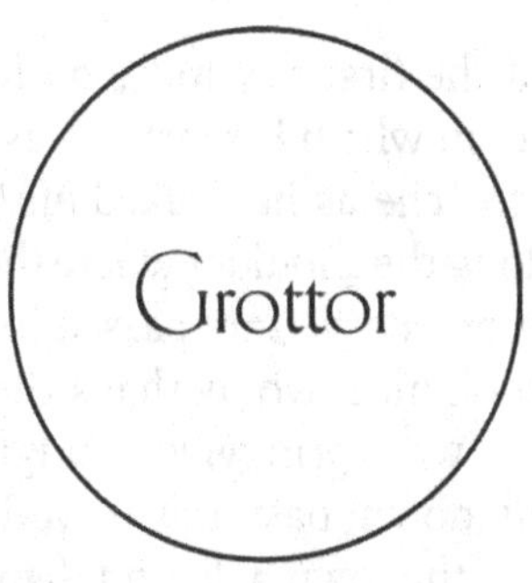

I.

At age thirteen, shortly after his father's death from tuberculosis and his mother's removal to the state facility for the insane, Bernt was given to his grandmother. His mother, he knew, wouldn't have wanted this – she had always done her best to keep him away from his grandmother, who she described as *not-right*, though without ever explaining what made her so. But his mother, straitjacketed, was not given a choice, was perhaps not even told: Bernt's court-appointed temporary guardian decided this was the option that best suited the state. *It will be*, the guardian declared, *the best for you as well.*

The following morning, before leaving for work, his ersatz guardian stationed Bernt near the curb to await his grandmother's arrival. When morning had become afternoon and she still hadn't arrived, Bernt decided to take matters into his own hands.

He travelled the first few miles on foot, passing the cemetery in which his father was buried. His feet began to ache as he walked out along State Route 89, along the shoulder where the gravel was fine, almost powdery. Cars passed him but none slowed. It took him two, perhaps three hours to reach downtown Springville, trudging up over the hill and down past the drive-in, past the grocery store, the town hall. And then he trudged back out the other side, watching the houses thin out and then be mostly replaced by fields. Houses appeared briefly again and he crossed through the four sorry streets of Mapleton, then more fields, nothing but fields. He drank alkaline-heavy water from a horse-pump, his stomach twisting on itself. The road's asphalt sputtered out, became gravel. His feet throbbed, were heavily blistered, perhaps bleeding.

Near dark, he stopped at a farmhouse and asked for directions. "The old woman?" the man who answered the door asked. "What do you want with her? Best to stay away." When Bernt admitted he was her grandson, the farmer stared thoughtfully at him. "Still better to stay away from her," he finally claimed, though in the end the man brought him inside and fed him, and then slipped on a jacket and drove him the rest of the way.

Bernt leaned his head against the truck's side window, feeling at once the burnt air of the heater blowing against his face and the way the glass itself was cooled by the night air outside. In the headlights he caught a glimpse of two small white crosses to the side of the road, almost hidden in the grass, and then they were gone.

The gravel road became dirt and then became rutted. Along the edge of the road was a running plain-wire line, two barbed top-wires above it. Bernt followed the fence mentally, its regular rhythm, until suddenly it turned a right angle and veered away from the road.

Another half mile and they were turning off the dirt road and pushing along the barest remains of a path, leaves and branches brushing the sides of the truck. They came to a ramshackle gate and stopped.

"She'll be back in there somewhere," said the farmer. "This is as far as I go." He reached over, patted Berndt's shoulder. "When you need help, you know where to find me."

~

He watched the broad front of the truck pull away, backing slowly up the path, its lights distancing, then reduced to a glow through the leaves, then vanishing altogether. He turned to the gate, tried to examine it in the moonlight. There was no latch; it was held in place by a twist of wire looped between the fencepost and the gate itself. He unhooked the wire, somehow slicing open his finger in the process. Sucking on the wound, he wondered how dirty the wire was, whether he needed a tetanus shot.

The land on the other side of the gate was uncultivated, nothing like a farm. There were no lights to suggest the location of a house and the path was sufficiently untraveled to be almost invisible in the darkness. He tried to follow it anyway, pushing his way forward through the grass and then, when he realized he'd misjudged in the darkness, backtracking, trying to find it again.

The moon slid behind a cloud and it became almost impossible to see. He did not know how long he'd been wandering when suddenly he was at the house, sensing it more than actually seeing it at first, and then, as the clouds shifted, catching a flash of the moon's reflection on one of the windows.

He managed to fumble his way to a door, and knocked on it. There was no answer. "Hello?" he called. He knocked again, still received no answer.

He groped around until he found the knob, then turned it, was surprised to find it unlocked. The door slid fluidly and silently open, and he stepped in.

~

The inside of the house was as dark as the outside had been, perhaps darker. He groped his way in, searching for a light switch without finding anything but a bare wall. Trailing one hand along it, he moved deeper into the house.

"Hello?" he called again.

He took a few more steps and then stopped, thinking he'd heard something. He waited a moment, listening, but the sound was not repeated.

He had just started moving again when he felt something flick quickly along his leg and away. He stumbled, nearly fell, gave an involuntary cry.

"No need to be frightened," said a soft, strangely warbled voice.

"Grandmother?" he said. "Where are you?"

The voice laughed. "I'm not your grandmother," it said. "I'm Grottor."

"Who?"

There was a scratching sound and a match blazed aflame. In its light Bernt saw, standing behind a table, a boy, roughly his height but very pale. He wore no shirt and his skin was tight to his bones, his muscles nearly as visibly articulated as an anatomy model's. Bernt watched the boy bring the match to a candle, holding it there until the flame caught and doubled itself, then letting the match fall, still smoldering, to the floor.

"Where's my grandmother?" Bernt asked.

"Your *mormor*?" said Grottor, and laughed. "You want to see your *mormor*?"

Before Bernt could ask what a *mormor* was, Grottor was gone, was leaving the entrance hall and sliding deeper into the house, vanishing in the darkness.

~

Not knowing what else to do, Bernt waited. There was something on the table other than the candle, a little pile of something that at first he thought to be strange irregular chunks of chalk but realized, once he came closer, were teeth. Four or five of them, almost certainly human.

He was reaching out to touch them when he heard a strange clumping sound and turned to see, lurching out of the darkness, an old woman. She was moving oddly, as if disoriented. She had an odd musty odor to her, strong even from a distance. She stopped at the doorway where she remained hunched over, staring down at the floor rather than looking at him.

"You're my *släkting*," she said. Her voice was strange, an unnatural falsetto, and seemingly too strong for her body.

"Excuse me?" he said.

"My flesh and blood," she said. Still staring at the floor, her mouth curled in a smile. "You have come to me."

"You were supposed to come get me," said Bernt.

"And yet here you are," she said. "My *släkting*," she said softly.

"Stop calling me that," said Bernt. "I don't know what it means."

The old lady nodded slightly, stiffly, as if offended. "There is a room for you," she said. "You may stay here. You may help."

"On the farm?"

"There is no farm," she said, "there are only the caves." She pushed her way out of the doorway and came closer until she was standing across the table from him. She reached out and jerkily stroked his hand, her skin leathery and stiff. "Grottor will take you there," she said. "You must trust Grottor. Trust Grottor in everything."

"Where is Grottor?" he asked. "What caves?"

She tightened her fingers around his hand and he was surprised to find her grip much stronger than he would have supposed. He winced. "Come," she said, "you may take the candle. There is a room for you. I will take you there."

II.

When he awoke, the day was half gone. His room, he saw now in the light coming in through the curtains, was small, the floor of bare, unvarnished boards. His bed was a simple cot. A rickety chair and his open suitcase were the only other furnishings in the room.

He got up, stretched. After getting dressed he wandered out, limping a little, his feet still sore from the walk.

Nobody greeted him. On the table in the entrance hall someone had left a tin cup of water and a skewer of smoked meat. The meat itself had an almost perfumed taste to it, and was very tough and stringy. He was hungry enough to eat it anyway.

The house itself, he saw by the light of day, was quite old and quite small. It consisted of an entrance hall, then a salon with two doors leading off of it: one to his room and the other to what was, presumably, his grandmother's room. In the back of the house, through the salon, was a small kitchen, its counters covered with a thick layer of undisturbed dust.

He tried the other door in the salon, found it locked. He knocked, but received no answer. "Grandmother?" he called, and then, as an afterthought, "*Mormor?*" Where, he wondered, was Grottor's room? Didn't Grottor live here too?

He went outside. He saw the path he had broken through the tall grass the night before. There was another path as well, this one well traveled, leading around to the back of the house. After a moment's hesitation, he followed it.

Once behind the house, this path quickly curved away and toward the mountain. He followed it a little way and then stopped. It switched back and up a slope, he saw, then crossed a flow of loose shale. There, up above the shale, were two dark openings, the entrances to a pair of caves.

Back in the house, he tried the door to his grandmother's room again. It was still locked. *Why does she keep it locked?* Bernt wondered. *Is she in there asleep or is she gone?* He limped outside again, tried to peer in his grandmother's window, but realized he had somehow walked around the house in the wrong direction and was now looking into his own window. There was his cot, his chair, his bloody socks, his small suitcase. He limped further around the house, and found the window of his grandmother's room to be shuttered. Through the slits in the shutters, he could see narrow rectangles of floor but little more. He pushed at the shutters a bit, but they were firmly latched from the inside.

~

The rest of the day was like that, a slow wandering through the house and around it, trying to figure out what to do with himself. He sat on the couch in the salon, thinking, the air thick with the smell of dust. Should he hike back down, talk to the farmer who had driven him here, try to get his advice on what to do? Should he beg someone to take him away from his grandmother?

He was still turning over such thoughts, vaguely ill at ease, when, late that afternoon, he found his eyes closing. Before he knew it, he had fallen asleep.

Suddenly, Grottor was standing above him, smiling. "Look," he said, and held out his hand to show Bernt three teeth. Canine, bicuspid, molar, each broken off roughly, above the root.

"Whose are they?" Bernt asked.

"Now they're mine," said Grottor.

"But whose were they?"

Grottor shrugged. "That's all that's left," he said, and then slipped out of the room.

~

He awoke in the fading light, in the slow onslaught of nightfall. Even after he woke up, after knowing he had been asleep, Bernt found he could not completely convince himself that Grottor's visit had been a dream.

He got up and found the matches where they lay on the entranceway table, looked through the mostly empty cabinets until he found a new candle.

By the time he got the candle lit, Grottor was there again, standing silently near the opening to the salon, still shirtless, startling Bernt when he turned.

"Don't you own a shirt? Where have you been?" Bernt asked.

Grottor just shrugged. "Here and there," he said.

"Where's my grandmother?"

"Your *mormor*? You want to see your *mormor*?"

And then Grottor turned and left the doorway. Taking up the candle, Bernt hurried to the entrance of the salon, arrived just in time to see him slip through his grandmother's door.

He went to the door, listened, heard nothing. He came closer, pressed his ear against the wood. Still nothing.

And then suddenly the door swung open and his grandmother stumbled out, almost knocking him over. She looked even stranger than she had before, was crumpled somehow, her skin loose and saggy. A strange smell rolled off her, like burnt hair.

"Ah," she said, in that same strange falsetto, still refusing to look up and meet his eye. "*Släkting*. You wanted me?"

"Um," said Bernt, still off-balance. "No," he said, "not exactly. Well, I wanted to know where you were all day."

His grandmother made a strangled sound that he decided must be a laugh. "For the day, I sleep," she said. "As do you. I command it. How are you to go to the caves at night if you do not sleep in the day?"

"What?" he said.

"Have you obeyed Grottor? Have you done everything that Grottor says, as I counseled you?" And then, without waiting for a response she placed a hand on his shoulder and pushed him away from the door to her room. She slipped back inside, closed the door.

What the hell? wondered Bernt. "Grand-mother?" he called and moved toward the door. He'd placed his hand on the doorknob, was about to turn it, when it opened of its own accord and there was Grottor. He tried to see past him to see his grandmother, but Grottor was already through the door and pulling it closed behind him.

"So, you've seen your *mormor*," said Grottor, rubbing his hands along his chest and arms as if dusting himself off. "What did the two of you talk about?"

"Do you share a room with her?" said Bernt. "Isn't that strange?"

Grottor just shrugged. "Enough chitchat," he said. "Now we go up to the caves."

~

Grottor gave him a flashlight and led him up the mountainside, on a steep dry climb to the caves. In the daylight the two openings had looked to Bernt small and shallow, two simple clefts in the rock, but they were higher up than he'd imagined, at the top of a steep, grand slide of shale, and were bigger too.

Up close, the first was a large, sideways bowl hollowed out as if by wind. Inside was a honeycomb of openings, each entrance just a little bigger than a man. All along the walls of the cleft were strange symbols, some painted in dark reddish-brown pigment, some scratched into the rock. There were images too; crude stick figures of men missing limbs or collapsed in a heap. A strange bulbous shape dominated one wall, beneath it a figure that seemed human but not human, strange rubbery appendages in the place of its limbs.

"What are they?" asked Bernt.

"Would you like to explore?" asked Grottor, ignoring the question. "Choose an entrance and we'll follow it in."

Bernt looked at him for a long moment, shook his head.

Grottor shrugged. "Next time, then. You've seen it at least. That's a start."

His eyes kept being draw to the bulbous shape and the humanoid figure. He had to make a conscious effort to free his gaze and look out of the cave. There, far away and below them, were lights of Mapleton: the real world. His grandmother's house, much closer but unlit, he could not see, nor even guess where it was.

Grottor stood up. "Come on," he said. "There's still the other cave to see."

~

They made their way along the face of the rock, walking on exposed shale that cracked and threatened to give way beneath their feet and send them tumbling down the slope and into the darkness. To bring himself to walk it, even in the dark, Bernt had to close his eyes, steady his hand on the rock wall. The second cave was less rounded than the first, like a mostly deflated ball, a sort of a sideways wavery slit in the rock, perhaps ten feet tall, twenty-five long. They clambered in.

Against the far wall, beside the one entrance to a tunnel, was a figure. Bernt went toward it, shining his flashlight. It was a body: an old woman, slight of frame, wearing old and frayed clothes. It had been dead a long time. The skin had been eaten away, the eyes were gone.

"Who is it?" Bernt asked.

"Who's what?" asked Grottor. "That? Don't worry about that, that's nothing."

"How can a body be nothing?"

"When it no longer holds a person," said Grottor flatly. "Then it's nothing."

"What's going on?" asked Bernt, a little hysterical now. "What did you do to her?"

Grottor just smiled.

Angry and confused, Bernt came at Grottor, arms out in front of him, but Grottor stepped quickly to one side, fading into the shadows. Bernt struck out, hitting only the rock wall, the sandstone grating against his knuckles. Grottor fell deeper and deeper into the shadows, slipping toward the back of the cave, always only imperfectly caught in the beam of the flashlight.

"Remember your grandmother?" said Grottor. "Remember what she said to you? You are to listen to me and pay me heed."

"How do you know what she said?" cried Bernt. "You weren't there."

And then Grottor's shadow, layered by other shadows, wavered over the opening of the tunnel at the back of the slit and was gone.

Bernt called out to him, but he did not answer. He moved all around the slit, shining his light, but Grottor had gone down the tunnel and was hidden now somewhere back in the caves, nowhere to be seen.

III.

At first he thought of just going, leaving, wandering down the mountain and disappearing. But as he shivered his way from one cleft to the other and then picked his way down the path, he began to ask himself, *Where would I go?* His father was dead, his mother insane, his court-appointed guardian didn't want him. Who else was there? Well, there was the farmer, the man who had given him a ride to his grandmother's, but how willing really was he to help? Did Bernt want to find out?

In any case, he told himself, coming closer to the house, his flashlight was dying. There was nothing to be done tonight. He would wait. In the morning, if he wanted, he could leave.

Later, back in his room, the moon came through the shutters to spread dim slats of light along his bed, the floor. Should he stay? Should he go? The dilemma was all around him, solid as architecture, like a structure he was forced to live in or a cage that was locked around his head. He was, he semi-consciously realized, slowly talking himself out of leaving – or at least *something* was, he thought with momentary panic, something wanted him to stay.

And then the panic left him as well and he was no longer certain what he'd been thinking about, what had happened in the caves or why he'd been worried.

~

He had uneasy dreams. His dreams took him backward along the path down the hill, through the farms, to Mapleton, then South. He walked for days, carrying a knife in his hand. He walked through desert and across blasted, blackened earth. He came to a border town, passed a boy whom he transformed into a corpse with his knife. As this transformation took place, he broke all the teeth out from the boy's mouth with the knife's haft. He turned the blade of the knife and the light caught on it and flashed across his eyes, and then he saw himself waver in the blade. Only it wasn't himself exactly, but who exactly it was he could not know.

~

He awoke to find Grottor staring at him, a shape in the darkness, a more tangible darkness. He wanted to be angry with him, but somehow

- 56 -

couldn't be, couldn't remember why he should be angry. He felt slowed, drugged.

"You've been dreaming," said Grottor. "A nightmare."

"Why is it still dark?"

"You slept through the daylight," said Grottor. "You're learning."

"Why won't you let me go?" Bernt asked.

He heard the hiss of a match, watched Grottor light the candle. "Go?" asked Grottor.

And then, suddenly, he remembered. "Did you kill the woman up in the caves?" asked Bernt.

"Would you believe me if I said I didn't?"

"You didn't?"

Grottor touched Bernt's lips with his finger. "Hush," he said. "You've had a nightmare. Go back to sleep."

"Why did you leave me alone in the caves?" asked Bernt.

Grottor shrugged. "Why are you thinking of leaving me?"

"That's different," said Bernt.

"Remember what your *mormor* said," said Grottor. "You must listen to me. Let yourself go and obey me."

~

How many days have I been here? he wondered, a few days or weeks later, and was puzzled to realize that he could not sort it out, not even roughly. A week or two at least, but perhaps a great deal longer than that, perhaps even years.

The dreams continued, filled with a host of people, none of whom he could place. With knives, he and Grottor forced these people up the side of the mountain, to the first of the caves. *Why only the first cave?* he wondered as he dreamt. They killed them there, drew circles around them in their own blood, inscribed their bodies with symbols whose meaning he did not know. Then they waited until something, a thing that he could never see, a kind of wavering shape that seemed imbued with the darkness between the stars, slowly dragged them back down one of the tunnels and away. What happened to them next, Berndt didn't know for certain: shortly after that he always woke up. It was not the killing itself, nor watching the bodies be dragged deeper in, which made him startle awake, but the realization that there was no shock, that it seemed smooth and natural from beginning to end, as if he had experienced the same thing a dozen times before.

Often he woke up to see Grottor in the room with him, sometimes even beside him in the bed, touching his lips, telling him *ssshhh*, that it was all just a dream. He did not know if it was worse to wake up like that or to wake up alone.

But it could be worse still. Several times, he had woken up not in his bed at all, but on the slope of the mountain, in full darkness, his body bruised and sore and he with no idea of where he had been.

Sometimes whole nights went by without him seeing his grandmother. On the nights when he did see her it was clear that there was something very wrong with her, something *not-right,* some sort of degenerative illness that was slowly transforming her. She could hardly control her limbs now. Her skin was flabby and hanging in some places, cracked and splitting in others. She no longer allowed him to come close, told him she did not want this to be how she remembered him.

She's dying, Bernt realized. *What will I do when she's dead?* He simultaneously felt worried and relieved. Maybe when she was dead he could work up the nerve to leave.

And then she turned slightly and he caught a flash of something, a rubberiness in her arms as if her bones had started to dissolve. It was so unnatural, he couldn't believe what he'd seen. He involuntarily took a few steps toward her.

"Do not approach!" his grandmother shrieked and just for a moment looked up and met his eyes, then moved swiftly through the door to her room, slamming it behind her.

Bernt had to lean against the wall to gather himself. What had he seen? Had he imagined it? No, he was certain he hadn't imagined it: he had seen the eyes not of an old woman but of a young boy. Grottor's eyes.

Quietly, he made his way to his *mormor*'s door. He kneeled, pressed his eye to the keyhole. The room was mostly dark inside, lit only by the glow of a solitary candle, but even in that dim light it was impossible to be mistaken. There was Grottor, stepping out of his grandmother's skin, like it was a suit of clothing. And there was Grottor, staring back at the door, staring right at the keyhole, a smile on his lips.

~

He fled. He ran down the mountain, veering on and off the road, listening for signs of pursuit. He knew what he had seen, but he also knew that if he told anyone he wouldn't be believed. What was he to do? Make up a story, something they would believe? Something, anything. He had to escape Grottor. He had to get away, as far away as he could.

~

He saw headlights far ahead, coming toward him, and he ran toward them, waving his arms. The truck, when it saw him, slowed, stopped.

"My grandmother," he said when the driver rolled down the window. "She fell and hit her head. She's dead." Only then did he realized it was the man who had first driven him to his grandmother's house.

"Dead?" said the man. "Are you sure she's dead?"

"I'm sure," said Bernt.

"Sometimes people look dead and they're not," said the man.

"She's dead," said Bernt.

"Well, get in already," said the man.

But once Bernt had climbed into the truck, he was surprised to find the man driving forward rather than turning around.

"Where are you going?" he asked.

"We have to make sure," said the man. "Just in case. You'd never forgive yourself if she was still alive and died because I didn't check."

And Bernt, not knowing what else to do, burst into tears. The man reached over and patted his shoulder, but kept driving toward his grandmother's house. Once the tears dried up, he shrunk against the side of the door and stayed there, hugging himself.

~

When they arrived, Bernt refused to get out of the car. *All right,* the man said, *that's understandable. You saw your grandmother fall and maybe die. I can understand why you don't want to go back in the house.* No, Bernt wanted to explain, it wasn't that, but something slowed his tongue and the man was too quickly gone.

He thought about running toward the house, somehow coaxing the man back before it was too late, but was afraid to leave the truck. He waited, feeling the darkness around him.

And then suddenly he was no longer alone in the truck. He knew that there was someone else there beside him, despite the fact that the door hadn't opened. He couldn't bear to turn his head to see who it was.

"Nice of you to oblige me by bringing a friend," said a voice that he knew to belong to Grottor.

Bernt tried to open his mouth, found his tongue cleaved to his palette. He made a strangled sound.

Grottor put his arm around his shoulder. He leaned closer until his eyes, shining in the darkness, were inches from Bernt's own. He could feel Grottor's warm breath against his face. "Who do you listen to?" asked Grottor in a way that made it clear the question was rhetorical. "Who is your god? Who is in charge of you now?"

IV.

Before the man was conscious again, Grottor and Bernt gagged him and bound his wrists tightly behind his back, running a lead off the rope as well. Then they went into the kitchen and got a knife, jabbing the man's arms with it until he woke up.

Bernt watched it all as it happened, unable to do anything but what Grottor wanted. He struggled, tried to break free, but couldn't. The man struggled too, and couldn't break free either.

They climbed the side of the mountain, following the path toward the caves. The beam of the flashlight was sharp, all things rendered crisp and in painful, explicit detail. Bernt watched, in front of him, the man struggling to climb, his bound wrists flexing against the small of his back. Bernt climbed behind him, the ground beneath his feet feeling distant, at a remove. Just behind him came Grottor.

They came to the top and entered the first cleft, though Bernt knew this was not where they would remain. They stopped, and the man stood, panting, his gag growing damp. The rope, Bernt could see, was chafing the skin away from the man's wrists. He watched Grottor lean against him, touching a finger to his gag.

"Hush," said Grottor.

The man tried to pull his head away.

He is going to kill him, thought Bernt, yet he could make no effort to stop him.

They made their way out of the cleft and along the face, over the bare, cracking rock. Bernt was first, looking back over his shoulder as he went, shining the light down at their feet. Grottor came behind, holding the man by an elbow to keep him from tumbling down the mountainside.

Bernt clambered up into the second cleft, then Grottor pushed the man up and came in himself. He jabbed the knife into the man's stomach, making him grunt. "Come on," he said, gesturing first at the man and then at Bernt. "Down the tunnel," he said, and held out his hand to take the flashlight.

Bernt went first, moving to the back of the slit. *There must a way out*, he was thinking, even though he couldn't stop walking. The man would die, there was no helping that, nothing he could do; Bernt had grown willing to sacrifice him if he himself could survive. Perhaps he could figure a way out. All he needed was some time.

But then he reached the back of the slit and stepped into the tunnel beyond. Behind him, Grottor's flashlight went dead and all around him the darkness grew palpable, quickly becoming more than he could stand. And then the flashlight came on again and he saw he had turned himself around in the tunnel somehow and was looking backward into the other man's pale and terrified face, at the mouth struggling against the gag.

"Keep going," said Grottor, so he did.

The tunnel grew narrow, its floor uneven. They started down a long incline and Bernt found the temperature rising around him, the air thick and hard to breathe. They went farther down, Bernt's feet now in tepid water which reached his knees. The passage began to tilt to one side so he had to lean and push off the rock below him, the other wall slanting to become the roof. Behind him, the man slipped. Though the passage was too narrow for Bernt to quite turn around, he could look back under one arm to see the man fallen on his face in the water and, with his hands tied behind his back, unable to get up. And then Grottor yanked the man up by the arms and he arose, water coursing down his face, and blood too, from where he had struck his forehead, but the gag still in place. Bernt could hear him coughing inside the gag, as if he were choking to death, water coming in gouts out of his nose. Grottor, steadying the man and helping him to angle his stance, flashed the light into Bernt's eyes, and said "Keep going." *I won't,* thought Bernt, but kept on.

The angle became severe, the passage tight enough that he had to lie on the slant floor, waist deep in water, and inch along on his back. The passage tightened further, the ceiling coming low enough to touch his chest. He had to let out his breath to move forward. He could no longer turn his head about so had to leave it to one side, looking backward at the man's damp and bloodied face, one hand feeling out blindly in front of him, Grottor's flashbeam behind him and darting all about. He could not see in front of him and could not tell where he was creeping, inch by inch. And then he wasn't creeping at all, for he saw the man behind him was no longer moving forward, his chest—

"What's wrong?" Bernt asked.

"He's stuck," said Grottor.

"Stuck?"

"You must be stuck too," said Grottor.

And Bernt suddenly knew that he was. He could feel the rock against his chest and his breath was with him only in short bursts and he could move neither forward nor back. For an instant, Grottor flicked the flashlight off and for Bernt there was nothing, not a thing, only an immense darkness, an asphyxiating nothingness. The flashlight came on again and he could see, in the light, the blood beating in the man's neck.

"This is enough," said Bernt. "Help me get free. Let's go back."

Grottor smiled. "Back," he said, using *mormor*'s falsetto.

Bernt closed his eyes and tried to think himself elsewhere, but when he opened them, the man was still there, and Grottor too, the latter pushing a knife along the upper edge of the wall, dragging one edge of it along the ceiling, bringing the other through the man's neck.

The man flinched and scraped the side of his head against the rock just above him, the knife cutting deeper. Grottor drew the knife back, the blood pulsing in little jets around it and then spreading in a sheet over the man's shoulders and down his chest. Bernt saw the man's throat tighten as he tried, under the gag, to swallow. Then the eyes, what he could see of them in the dim light, began to glaze. They turned opaque and Bernt knew the man was dead.

He could see through the cleft in the man's neck a section of Grottor's face, the single visible eye pale and hard. Grottor was reaching out with one hand, fingering the man's neck, his sodden shirt.

He began smearing the rock above with the man's blood, writing vague symbols, muttering as he did so.

"What are you doing?" asked Bernt.

"Now it will come for him but take you too. All I need is your skin. Your *mormor* is worn out: who better to replace her than her *släkting*?"

And then his hand was withdrawn and Bernt could hear Grottor's body scraping its way back down the tunnel and away, the light of the flashbeam ever more distant. He called out, found no response. The other man's face in the dying light was a solid mass, another rock, inscrutable. *Don't leave me*, Bernt called to Grottor, but there was no response.

He closed his eyes. When he opened them it had fallen dark all around him, darker than he could bear, and then, somehow, it grew darker still.

He waited, mind slowly collapsing, for the darkness to take him.

I.

In early Spring, Harmon's sister disappeared. One moment she was standing at the edge of the property, near the back fence, the dog just beside her, listening to him plough. The next, both she and the dog were gone. He noted their absence passively as he turned the tractor to cut the next set of rows, and thought nothing of it. Later, once he was done, he went into house and called, was surprised when neither she nor the dog came. The dog he found a half-day later, just outside the back fence, its throat slit open. Of his sister, however, there was no sign.

~

He tramped the farmlands for miles, knocking on every door he could find. He drove into town, asked around at the co-op and the bar. When it was clear nobody there had seen her he finally drove two towns north and to the sheriff's office.

"How long has she been gone?" asked the deputy on duty.

Two days, Harmon told him.

The deputy looked him over. "That's not so long," he said. "Usually we wait a while to make sure they don't come back on their own."

"They?" he asked.

"She in this case," said the deputy. "Was there any trouble between you and your wife?"

"What?" said Harmon, confused. "But I don't have a wife."

"Your girlfriend, then," said the deputy. "Whatever you call her."

"She's my sister," said Harmon.

"Your sister?" asked the deputy, and Harmon saw his gaze sharpen. "You live with your sister?"

There was nothing wrong with a man in his forties living with his sister, Harmon tried to explain.

"I never said there was," said the deputy, pursing his lips. "Your sister, then," he said. "Just the two of you?"

Yes, Harmon admitted, just the pair of them.

"Maybe she just wanted to get away for a while," suggested the deputy. "Out on her own."

Harmon nodded, then explained about the murdered dog.

"That does sound bad," said the deputy. "But maybe it's something else."

"Something else?"

"Maybe it's a separate incident. Are you sure it's the same incident?"

"She was there with just the dog and then she disappeared," said Harmon, trying not to lose his temper. "The dog disappeared too, and when it reappeared it was slaughtered. That's worth looking into."

"Did you bring a picture?" the deputy asked Harmon.

"Of the dog?" asked Harmon.

"Of the sister," said the deputy.

Well, no, Harmon admitted. In fact as far as he knew there was no picture.

The deputy looked astonished. "No picture?"

"Maybe when she was a baby," said Harmon, "but I never seen one even then."

"That's okay," said the deputy, offering a fake smile. "We can work around that. What'd she look like?"

"I don't know," said Harmon. He shrugged. "Ordinary, I guess."

"Tall or short," asked the deputy.

Harmon shrugged again. "Normal height, I guess."

"Hair color," said the deputy.

"Maybe brown," said Harmon.

"So, brown?"

"Maybe," said Harmon.

"What do you mean, maybe?"

"I'm blind to colors," said Harmon. "Some colors anyway. Sometimes I can guess. Others I just can't tell."

"Didn't you ever ask her?"

Harmon shook his head. "Never had a reason to," he said.

The deputy shook his head. "What about her eyes?" he asked.

"Didn't really have a color," said Harmon.

"No? You couldn't see their color?"

Harmon shook his head. "They didn't really have one. They were filmed over and milky. Opaque. That's why she had the dog."

"Excuse me?"

"She didn't really venture anywhere without the dog," said Harmon. "She couldn't much," he said. He looked up at the deputy. "How could she? She was blind."

~

The deputy's attitude changed with that; suddenly he started taking Harmon more seriously. Another deputy followed him back to the farm and listened to him talk about the moment his sister had vanished. He showed the man around the house; the meager kitchen, the bathroom, the single bedroom with the two twin beds in it pressed up against opposite walls, a curtain strung between them. The deputy didn't seem to want to come into the bedroom, just watched from the door as Harmon rummaged through the boxes under one bed and then the boxes under the other, looking for a photograph. There wasn't one.

A few hours later, the deputy had called out a trio of bloodhounds. They were given one of the sister's skirts to smell and then went crisscrossing their way over the dirt until one picked up the scent and started baying. It took off, the others following.

"Looks like we're in luck," said the deputy.

Harmon felt his heart thudding up inside his throat. They set out after the dogs and their handler, only to end up at the spot behind the fence where Harmon had found his own slaughtered dog.

They tried again, then a third time, but the dogs kept returning to the same spot, losing the scent there. After a while the handler led them back to the truck and drove them away.

"Try not to think the worst," the deputy told him a few minutes later, clapping a hand on his shoulder. Harmon had to stop himself from asking what the worst might be. A moment later, he felt the hand lift. Soon the deputy was gone as well.

~

What if I'd stopped when I first noticed her gone? he couldn't help but think, late at night, staring at the curtain hanging limply between him and his missing sister. *What if I'd looked for her then, what would I have found?*

But how could he know? Could he really have saved her? From what? Mightn't whatever it was simply have come for him too, as it apparently had for the dog?

Then it was morning and he was up, getting on with the planting, trying not to think about her. He couldn't, on top of everything else, lose the crop before he'd even begun. He didn't stop for lunch, which normally his sister would have made for him. *She can't have run off*, he thought, *not blind*. But who, then, had taken her? Hard not to think of her as having gone the way of the dog, her throat slit open, her body dead in some dry creek bed somewhere. Was that what the deputy had meant by the worst? He shook his head to try to rattle the thought out of it.

Once the light went bad, he stopped and drove into town. He asked again about her at the co-op, but they just shook their heads. He went into the bar and had a beer, asked the bartender if he'd heard anything.

"No," said the bartender, shaking his head. "No news, sorry."

When Harmon had finished his beer, he couldn't stop himself from going around from customer to customer, asking the same question. *No*, they all said. They hadn't seen her, hadn't heard of anybody who claimed they had.

What now? he wondered, out on the street again. He thought for a moment, but when nothing came to him he went home and went to bed.

~

That night, he had a dream. In the dream it was not that his sister was missing, but that he'd never had a sister. Or at least that was how he interpreted it. In the dream, he was lying in his bed in his half of the room, staring at the curtain that split the room in half. He got up and pulled the curtain back and there, instead of the other half of the room, was only emptiness and darkness.

When he came groaning awake, it took a long time for him to gather himself. He lay in the bed, staring at the curtain. Finally he got up and drew it back, only to find the other half of the room as it has always been: the dismal mirror of his own half.

~

Finishing the first round of planting alfalfa, more preparations. The linear-move sprinklers going now as well, on their huge carapace, which made its slow creaking path forward on the swollen wheels. It reached the end of the rows and then had to be reset, sent back again. Always something to do, always more planting or a fence to be mended or something gone wrong with the tractor. Then evenings back into town, inquiring again about his sister: the co-op, the bar. That single beer, all he could really afford, though sometimes the bartender took pity and poured it half-full for him again. Making the slow round of customers, watching them each shake their heads no, then back out into the night to wonder, feeling a little dazed, *What now? What next?*

~

Until one night, maybe ten days after her disappearance, maybe fifteen, the bartender, instead of simply saying *No*, instead of simply saying *No news*, leaned his elbows on the bar and said "Where else you tried, Harmon?"

"Co-op," said Harmon. "And the sheriff."

"I didn't mean where'd you ask," said the bartender. "I meant where'd you look?"

Where *had* he looked? He'd driven around a bit, looked around town, looked in the land around his farm.

"What about the caves?" the bartender asked. "Or the old Glave place?"

Harmon stayed motionless a moment, then nodded and went out. *The caves, no*, he thought as he got into the truck and drove. There were always teenagers in them, messing about. If she was there, she'd have been found already. But the Glave place, well, that was a thought. How had he not thought of it before?

II.

It was a long slow drive, through the farms and then up into the foothills, following the old road that edged the river. The road was rough and washed down in places, potholed and jagged with rocks in others. It was already late, or at least late for Harmon, the sky grown dark, the road ahead lit indifferently by the truck's single working headlight. He moved slowly forward, following the river road, the sound of the river always in his ears.

He came to a place where the road was blocked, a large, rotted tree having fallen across. He pulled the truck up close to it and stopped, getting out to take a look. He tried to shift it with his hands, then got back into the truck to try to prod it out of the way with his bumper. But the tree was a little too low and the truck's bumper kept threatening to surge over it and get stuck.

He turned off the truck and climbed out, first fumbling an old flashlight out of the glove box. He turned it on, shook it a little until the bulb lit feebly up, then climbed over the fallen tree, continued on.

He came to a fence, a series of long metal stakes strung with four strands of barbed wire, triple-prong. Had that been there the last time he'd been up to the Glave place? Maybe, or another fence perhaps. That had been years ago, just after the last Glave's suicide, back when Harmon was a child. And he hadn't stayed long, had been eager to leave. The sign, though, forbidding trespassing, that was new, or at least freshly painted. There was a gate, there, where the road continued, but it was padlocked shut.

Standing on the first and second wire, he pulled the third up and wriggled his way through. A barb got caught up in his hair, tore a chunk of it free. When he was through and went to lift up his foot, he found his boot stuck, a barb sunk deep into the sole. He pulled it free, continued on.

There was the Glave house, just up the slope, still too far away for the flashlight to illuminate, a kind of intense darkness couched in an immense, lesser darkness. The flashlight flickered, went out. Walking in the dark, he patiently jiggled it until the bulb illuminated again, then held it carefully, awkwardly, like it was a glass too full of water – which made him picture himself, just for a moment, back in his own house, carrying a glass of water to his sister's bedside table, on the way to bed. He shook his head. There was the Glave house now, the angles and edges coming slowly out of the darkness, becoming hard.

A series of steps, rough-carved blocks of granite. What was it that Glave had been? Harmon tried to remember. As a kid, Harmon had known, or been told something. Why couldn't he recall? And why had Glave killed himself? Did anyone know? And why this house, here, high in the hills, on the slope of the mountain, a grand distance from everything? *Doesn't matter*, Harmon tried to tell himself, and pushed his way up the uneven steps and to the door.

Inside, the floor had collapsed in places, though in others it seemed solid enough.

Carefully he shined the flashlight round the front hall, calling out for his sister. There was no answer. A set of stairs wound up to almost the level of his head, but the top rungs were missing, leaving a good man's height between the end of the stairs and the opening in the ceiling above. He called out again, then moved slowly forward, testing the floor before him as he went. The flashlight flickered and went out, then came on again.

A door – a hall, the floor better here. He moved forward down it, looking through doorways into ruined rooms, scatterings of broken glass, char-marks from cook-fires, bits and pieces of unrecognizable furniture. Otherwise empty. A final door at the hall's end – *probably the back door of the house*, he thought. But he opened it anyway.

~

It was not the mountainside the door opened onto, but another room, a huge vaulted chamber impossibly large for what he'd been able to discern in the dark (and in the darkness of memory) about the size of the house. The floor was intact and seemed solid. It was freshly scrubbed: he could smell the odor of ammonia and resin rising off it. The walls were covered with thick, dark curtains which, in the waver of the flashlight's beam, appeared almost, but not quite, black. The cupola of the vault was pierced by a few narrow windows, which did little to lessen the darkness. The room was thickly furnished, cluttered with a sea of empty wing-backed chairs and fainting couches, the pattern of their brocade faded. The air seemed exceptionally cold, much colder than it had been outside.

At the room's far end was a large desk, dark wood, perhaps mahogany, behind which was seated a man. He was old, his eyes pale but his gaze sharp. When the beam of the flashlight touched him he did not move, though his eye flicked up to gaze into it. He wore a dark suit, Harmon saw, tightly buttoned, though his tie was undone and hung loose from the collar. The man's face itself was pale, but its lines were firm, almost young, the gray hair combed back tight against his skull. Harmon played the light over his face for a moment before letting it shine around his own feet.

"Yes?" the old man asked, his lips hardly seeming to move as he spoke.

Harmon cleared his throat but found he could not speak.

They both waited, silent. At last the old man moved, if only slightly. He tightened his lips, narrowed his eyes.

"You're Harmon," the man said.

"Yes," Harmon managed.

"Thought so," said the old man. "We've met before, if I'm not mistaken."

Harmon turned the flashlight back on the old man again. Did he look familiar? Where would they have met? But if they hadn't met, how had the old man known his name?

He was still staring when his flashbeam flickered, went out.

He shook it softly but it didn't come back on. *It doesn't mean anything,* he reminded himself, feeling his mouth go dry. *It was doing that before.*

"And to what," asked the old man's voice from the darkness, "do I owe the pleasure?"

"My sister," Harmon finally managed.

"What is it about your sister?" asked the voice, patient, cold.

Harmon shook the flashlight again, without result. "She's missing," he said.

"Missing is she," said the voice. "Why are you telling me?"

"I want her back," said Harmon.

"What makes you think *I* have her?" asked the old man.

Harmon opened his mouth then closed it again. Did he think that? No, not exactly, but he was not sure what exactly he thought. Finally, he said, "You're the only one I haven't asked."

There was a long silence. For a moment it felt to Harmon as if the room had dissolved around him, a vast darkness opening up. But then he began to see, in the slight light seeping in through the vault, the ghosts of the chairs, the vague shape of the old man.

~

"Let me tell you a story," the old man finally said, his voice lower now. "Or maybe two stories. Unless it's just one story with two different endings.

"Perhaps you've heard it, Harmon. The way the story usually goes is like this. A man has a wife who, for whatever reason, dies, struck down in the so-called blossom of her so-called youth. The man loves her deeply so decides, blind with longing, to bring her back from the dead. Accordingly, he descends. Through his wiles or his skill he coaxes his way deeper and deeper down until he strikes a deal with death. There are complications, but in the end he leads his wife back to the world of the living. Are you with me, Harmon? Have you heard this story?"

"I don't know," said Harmon.

"You don't know?" said the man. "You've heard it now, more or less."

"Do you know her?" asked Harmon. "Do you know my sister?"

"Just listen," said the voice. "Just because a story is told the same way over and over doesn't mean that that's the way it happened."

"No?" said Harmon.

"No," said the old man. "But it also doesn't meant that it *didn't* happen that way either," said the old man.

"I don't understand," said Harmon, helplessly.

"Exactly," said the old man. "Just listen.

"There are two other ways we might tell the story," he said. His eyes now, Harmon saw, were catching the slight light, and were little glistening spots in the darkness. "Shall we, Harmon? Are we really the sort of men to be satisfied with the story everyone else is telling?

"One of the other versions is almost the same. Our hero, loving deeply, descends ready to wrest our heroine from the hands of the dead. He confronts and surmounts the obstacles along his path and strikes a deal with death. He may take his wife – or if you prefer his sister – with him, but he must not look at her until he reaches the realm of mortals. So, he takes her blindly by the hand and leads her, his eyes closed, back the way he came, out of the land of the dead. All has gone well, he hasn't looked once and there he is at last, solid mortal ground under his feet. And so he turns and embraces his wife, his sister, and opens his eyes to see her at last.

"Only it's not her at all. He's brought back the wrong girl."

"Why would you tell me that?" asked Harmon.

"The other version," said the voice, rising slightly, "goes much the same. He's allowed to bring her back and this time she's still his sister, his wife, whatever. Only the thing is that just because she's come back from the land of the dead, doesn't mean she's any less dead herself. She's still dead, only she's alive too. Both living and dead. Which, take it from me, Harmon, is hardly a pleasant combination for anyone."

There was silence for a moment, then a slow rasping sound from the darkness, a sound that Harmon couldn't place. It made one of side of his face tighten, hearing it, and for a moment his heart felt like it had stopped beating. He took a step sideways, his hip knocking against a chair or some other piece of furniture.

"But what about you, Harmon?" asked the voice from the darkness. "How do you think your story is likely to end? Do you really care to find out?"

III.

He awoke with a start, as if drowning. There was the taste of dirt in his mouth and dirt on his face as well, and he was lying just outside the ruined house, just outside the Glave place, chilled to the bone.

The sky was just starting to lighten. He pulled himself to his feet, the bones in his hands and feet aching with cold. Carefully he circled the house, started down the slope, down the dirt road, over the locked gate, slowly making his way back to his truck.

He was back at his farm before the sun rose. He fried a thick slice of bacon, then added three eggs to the spattering grease. As he ate, he couldn't help but think of the dog, its throat slit, its body slung in the dirt. Nor his sister either, of the times when her breathing had grown regular and he had stood and parted the curtain between them, watching her sleep in the pale light cast by the night.

There was work to be done, the alfalfa and other crops to be inspected, a place where the linear-move sprinkler had gotten stuck and had left the ground swampy. A jackrabbit trapped in the barbed wire of the back fence, slowly dying. He slit its throat then felt its ribs and legs to decide if it might be worth cooking, finally leaving it hanging there as a warning to the others. It was all coming along, he thought, not good and not bad but coming along, probably well enough to make it through another year.

Then, before he knew it, the day was gone. He was exhausted, worn out by the events of the day itself and all that had happened the night before. He found a cured sausage, rolled in flour, dangling in the back of the pantry. He cut it in half, putting one half in the rattling fridge, the other on a plate. He ate it slowly, with hard, stale crackers and mouthfuls of water.

I should go into town, he thought, *and ask about her.* Instead, he sat there at the table, staring at his empty plate, until he realized he was falling asleep.

~

At first he slept deeply, without dreams – or at least without any dreams he could remember. Then he began to dream vividly, dreams that seemed more or less like the life he was living, except that his sister was there now, always beside him. Though in the dream it was as if he was someone else, watching both himself and his sister through a thick pane of glass. The Harmon in the dream somehow couldn't see his sister, didn't know she was there. So, he went to town in search of her, the sister feeling her way along just behind. She was there just beside him as he ate, she was standing on the edge of the fields listening to him plough. At night she stood there beside him, looming over his bed, staring down at him with her sightless eyes, staring, unseeing and blinking, down at him.

~

He awoke in the dark, shaking. Slowly he willed himself to calm down. *Just a dream*, he told himself, *nothing but a dream*.

He was still lying there, staring up into the darkness, trying to fall back asleep, when suddenly he began to hear it. A slow, steady scratching, from just outside, from just the other side of the wall. What was it? Abruptly it stopped. Then just as he was beginning to relax it started again. *What is it?* he wondered, *Who?* – though he quickly realized that perhaps the answer to this was something he did not want to know.

He lay there, both terrified and elated, listening to the slow scratching, wondering what his life would be like from here on out, putting off for as long as possible the moment when he would have to get up and go find out.

...la peste la plus terrible est celle qui ne divulgue pas ses traits.

    —Antonin Artaud, *Le théâtre et son double*

I.

They were to travel due South, checking fenceline for \$2/day to territory's extreme, and then to cross over and observe conditions beyond. They rode by horse, seeing only perfect and secure fence to either side of the road until, near the border, the landscape grew ribbed and strange. It was not merely stony but gnarled all through like a brain, and soon even the road grew awkward and folded beneath the horses' hooves.

Near midmorning of the third day, Hunt's gelding stumbled, lurched down. When they tried to coax it up they discovered its forequarters coursed over with blood. They searched for a wound but there was none, only blood rising like sweat to the skin's surface, matting the hair. The animal breathed shallow and restless until Hunt, not knowing what other course to take, fired a bullet through its eye. The animal convulsed, fell still.

Hunt slit the animal's belly with his hip-knife, spilled the stomach's contents upon the ground, smeared them about, regarded them askance for irregularity. He parted the animal's throat with his knife's barb, peered in. Peeling the hide back from the forequarters in a dripping sheet, he unfurled it between himself and the sun, looking for lesion or other hidden wound.

"What have you found?" Haish asked him.

"Naught but ordinary horse," said Hunt, casting the hide aside. Wiping his knife on his pant leg, he sheathed it, began to walk.

Haish and Grenniger dismounted, bridle-led the two horses that remained. By noon, Hunt was bleeding too, dim drops of blood-fluxed fluid gathering in the corners of his eyes. Grenniger noticed first. Then Hunt himself seemed to notice in wiping the back of his hand across his face. Grenniger grabbed Haish by the shirt and held him behind. They watched Hunt's black shirt grow damp and dark, but could not see what was blood and what sweat until he turned and they saw his boot-tips pizzled over with blood, with more blood obscuring the better part of his face. Haish tugged the rifle from Grenniger's saddle-holster and shot Hunt through one shoulder and then, as he came closer, his wounded arm hanging limp, shot him through the temple. Hunt fell, brimming ordinary blood, his brains smearing into the ground.

They did not touch Hunt's corpse. Out of fear or prudence they tightened handkerchiefs across their faces then shot and killed their own horses, leaving the carcasses untouched and unexamined.

They continued on foot, faces sweating into the cloth. By mutual consent, they kept to opposite edges of the road, Grenniger carrying the rifle and wearing the provisioned saddlebag slung over one shoulder, Haish with the notebook and saddlebags of his own, both with the pockets of their longcoats rattling with bullets.

~

Two days later they arrived at the border station, a warp-wood structure backed with a dilapidated barn. When they knocked, nobody answered. The windows were too filthy and dark to peer properly through, and the little Grenniger could see seemed a ruin.

"And now?" asked Haish.

Grenniger rattled the door's knob, then stepped back off the porch and regarded the door.

They both walked around the building, to the barn behind. There was a bad smell about the place. They knotted their handkerchiefs tighter into their faces. Through the slats of the two stalls nearest to them, they could see dead horses, their bodies picked apart by birds, some of which lay fallen near them, dead as well. The straw was rusty with dried blood. Protruding from the farthest stall was a pair of new boots, a pale portion of leg tucked into them.

"Boots," called Haish. "Still alive?"

When no answer came, they left the barn.

"We turn back," said Haish. "Inform the company of the contagion."

"We submit a report," said Grenniger. "The company determines whether we turn back or push forward."

"Are you planning to submit it to Boots back there?" Haish asked. "He's all you have."

Shaking his head, Grenniger pointed to the telegraph wires stretching away from the station.

He rattled the station's door again, then leaned hard into it. It creaked in the frame. Stepping back, he kicked it. The frame splintered out at the lock, the knob rolling crippled loops about the porch.

The room smelled thick with smoke, the air catching in their throats. The center of the floor was scorched with ash and charred lumber-ends, ceiling and walls streaked black. Several chairs had been broken up, the wood tossed into a corner unburnt. A large safe lay turned on its side but unopened, attached by an iron chain to a ring in the floor. A door in the far wall had a board nailed across it.

"Hardly promising," said Haish.

"Shut up," said Grenniger. He moved slowly about the room, peering about, wiping his finger through the wall's ash, then moved toward the door.

"We turn back," said Haish.

"We do not know which direction the contagion is moving," said Grenniger. "It might be safer to move ahead."

He drew his knife, worried the blade between the board and the door, pried carefully until the nails started to come loose. Sliding the knife free, he forced the blade under the head of each one in turn, the nails loosening while their heads curled up and threatened to break off. When the board's end was loose enough to get his fingers around, he braced his foot against the wall and pulled. It wrenched free, nails screeching and coming out warm to the touch.

Behind the door sat a small table, a telegraph apparatus screwed onto it. Beside, on the floor, was a man, his shirt swollen with blood, breath tugging out of him ragged.

Grenniger nudged the man's foot with the nail-puckered board.

The man's head stirred, rising slightly. They watched his eyes focus on them then turn back in the sockets, his head flopping down again.

"Take the money," he said, breathing a little between each word, his eyes now closed. "Combination beneath the desk."

"What?" said Haish. "No," he said, fingering the handkerchief over his face. "Pay no attention to this. We aren't bandits."

"How long have you been here?" asked Grenniger.

"I don't know," said the man.

"How long have you been sick?" Grenniger asked. He had to repeat the question before he was convinced the man had understood.

"We must send a message," said Grenniger. "Do you still remember your Morse?"

The man moved his lips a little.

They took off their boots and snaked them over their hands and forearms, and then, protected, attempted to make the telegraph operator comfortable. They tried at first to sit him in the chair but he had lost control of his body, could now move little more than his head, could not lift his hands at all. Spreading him back along the floor, they slipped on their boots again.

At Grenniger's persistent prompting, the man eventually came to relay to them the telegraph code, telling them in patches how to send, to listen. Haish rendered it in the last page of the notebook.

contagion stop hunt dead stop horses dead stop station ruined stop please advise stop

It grew dark outside. They lit the kerosene lamp on the desk beside the telegraph and waited, Haish rolling a cigarette and lifting his handkerchief off his face long enough to smoke it. They listened to the telegraph officer's irregular breathing.

"The bastard gets under my nerves," said Haish, stubbing his cigarette on his boot-heel. He pulled the handkerchief back over his face again. "Breathing like that."

Grenniger shrugged.

After a while, Haish got up and took the rifle from beside Grenniger, shot the man through the chest. He sat down again, crossed his arms.

"He is still alive," said Grenniger after a time.

"It doesn't matter," said Haish. "As long as he don't breathe like that again."

"Would Hunt be alive if we hadn't shot him?"

"Would Hunt want to be?"

They sat staring at each other, then at the lamp. Grenniger got up and shot the man again, then a third time to make sure he was dead. Haish smoked another cigarette, grinding it out on the desktop when he was through. He got up and went to the other room, came back with a second lamp, lit its wick off the first, then was gone again with it. Grenniger watched him crouch, peering at the underside of the desk. Then he disappeared to the other side of the room.

Grenniger listened to him, the click of the lock then the safe door swinging, then silence. He closed his eyes and rubbed them. When he opened them again, Haish was back in the room, seated beside him.

"There was money?"

"No."

"What was there?"

"See for yourself."

Taking one of the lamps, Grenniger walked to the other room. The safe door was slightly ajar, a hand spilling out the opening, palm up. Slipping a chair leg from the pile in the corner, he levered the door open.

Inside was a corpse, curled up, legs heavily bruised, lips blue. He prodded the hand back in, closed the safe, made sure it locked.

He stepped onto the porch for air and found himself walking first around the house and then out to the barn. He moved slowly, lifting the lamp high to peer at the dead or dying animals in each stall. Most, he saw, seemed not to have died of the contagion itself, but of a gunshot. Making his way to the last stall, the one with the boots in it, he peered in. The man was still alive, breathing a little.

"Hey," said Grenniger. "Boots."

No sign of acknowledgment. Grenniger raised the lantern higher. One side of the man's neck was covered with a seething pale grubwork, the flesh beginning to pucker off.

"Can you hear me?" Grenniger asked.

When the man did not answer, Grenniger took a shovel off the wall, used it to push the man's head around. He shouted to him to wake up. When he did not, Grenniger brought the blade of the shovel down hard against his forehead. He kept hitting until the head grew soft. Soon the breathing stopped.

Inside, Haish had the receptor near his head, was frantically writing dots and dashes. Grenniger sat down beside him. He watched him finish, then aided him in transforming Morse to words.

pursue contagion along fenceline stop else all monies forfeit stop

II.

Once across the border, the fence changed. The posts, of an insufficiently salted Douglas fir, were windcarved to a deep grain. The barbing consisted of the usual two-point triple-coil barb on a plain two-strand wire, but the barbs were clumped along the wire in triads rather than spread singly.

They followed the fence, looking for breakage or slack wire or decayed posts. There were no animals, no sign of people either, though the wire itself had been recently and awkwardly hand-repaired. Between posts, the barbs were altogether absent.

Haish wrote in the notebook: *Arched-strand, trebly grouped. Two-strand wire, two-point barb, triple-coil, commercial manufacture, hand-repair.*

The saddlebags kept sliding from his shoulder as he tried to write. He sketched a portion of the barbed strand. He counted posts as he walked, scoring a hash at the bottom of the page at what he roughly judged was every mile.

To either side, dull brush and sage. A mountain at some distance to the East, the road thick with dust. A river visible at some little distance from the road, slow and lazy. Nothing living to be seen.

Nothing alive, Haish inscribed, then added, as an afterthought, *except us.*

"We should turn back," he suggested, closing the notebook. "Money be damned."

Grenniger seemed not to have heard.

"Forget the money," said Haish. "I will offer you money out of my own pocket."

Grenniger nodded, but kept walking. The road threaded quietly through low hills, the fence running alongside. The land was beginning to buckle up and they could see mountains far ahead, purple for distance.

"I am going back," said Haish.

"I won't stop you," said Grenniger, without slowing.

Haish dropped a few paces back. *I worry about Grenniger,* he wrote in the notebook, though he knew he had not been given the notebook to worry about Grenniger.

At the bottom of a hill the lowest wire of the fence ran slack and was covered briefly by silt or other alluvia, the fence so low as to serve as little deterrent to beings within or without.

"Shall we fix it?" asked Haish.

"Wrong side of the border," said Grenniger. "We observe. We record. We don't meddle."

When night fell, they started a fire with tumbleweed and the driest sage, smoke rising pungent enough to make their eyes water until they began to feed scrub oak in. Seated on opposed sides of the fire, they regarded one another.

"What are we searching for?" asked Haish. "What does a source of contagion resemble?"

"You know as well as I."

"I don't know anything."

Grenniger pushed his hat back. "Neither do I," he said.

"That isn't sufficient."

"It shall have to serve."

Haish got up, sat back down again.

"You may leave at any time," said Grenniger. "I am not holding you here."

"You want me to leave?"

"Not at all."

"Tell me you want me to stay."

Grenniger snorted. "I'm not your lover," he said. "Leave or stay: it won't break any heart but your own."

~

The fence changed and Haish promptly recorded it in his book. *Double-strand undulate wire, coldweather, armatured with Glidden's coil.* At regulated intervals, the wire was hung with thin reflective squares of sheet metal that flung the light back. When Haish touched them, he found them cooler than the wire itself. Puzzled by what to write, he left only a blank line. He walked several thoughtful miles before opening the book again to designate them *Galvanized warning squares, home-made.*

He had walked another mile before realizing his thumb ached. Looking down, he realized he still held the book, thumb slipped between pages.

What are we searching for exactly? he wrote.

What might we have to learn from wire? Is it better revealed here, across the border, among new varieties, hand-patched? What is the connection between wire and contagion, if any? When will I die?

He knew he was entering a speculative space he should shy from, that the notebook would seem, to anyone who read it later, indication of a delirium. Yet he could not stop writing. As certain as he was that he should not write them, he was also convinced the questions were necessary.

He wrote: *What is Grenniger hiding?*

"What are you writing?" asked Grenniger.

"Recording fence," Haish said, scratching the sentence out.

When, a few miles further, Grenniger was again paying him no heed, Haish wrote: *What are the qualities and properties of wire that one might see as essential? Firstly, wire runs in a strand. Secondly, wire can be used to make fences or other sorts of constricting structures. Thirdly, wire expands and contracts with weather. Fourthly, wire fences, if not set correctly or not composed of a properly twisted double-strand, may snap or sag.*

How can I make anything of that? Haish wondered, staring at the notebook.

The road navigated a lazy series of curves, ascending the side of a worn half-mountain. The mountain had eroded into shelves of shale, the road becoming a path, then no more than a track, awkward and narrow and crumbling. Haish tucked the book into his shirt.

The fence followed alongside them most of the way up, then turned abruptly away at a right angle. They kept climbing, breathing heavily. The sun slipped in the sky, boiled down to a dull red, then disappeared altogether. With their boots, they dug the path deeper into the face, dragged the ground to try to even it. They lay down in a line, feet to feet, not quite touching. Haish opened his saddlebags, felt around until he found a strip of jerky.

"How much food do you have left?" asked Grenniger.

"A few days' worth. Water for one."

"We'll find water."

"Perhaps," said Haish.

Grenniger grunted softly in the dark, a sound Haish could just hear above the straining of his jaw against the dried and striating meat.

"We're likely to die of it?" Haish asked.

Grenniger did not respond.

"Would it matter to you if we died?" Haish asked.

He heard Grenniger turn and settle in the dark, smelled the dust his turning brought up. He pushed his saddlebags around, settling his head on them.

He lay thinking, wishing he had his notebook out and was sure enough of himself to write in the dark. He wasn't sure what he would write. He was falling asleep and as he did he imagined shoving Grenniger off the path and down the mountainside. Grenniger was pitching and sliding, then dead, tongue lolling, and then Grenniger was back on the path and he was pushing him off again. He saw it so many times in succession that it began to acquire the character of a memory. He slid down a little, stretched his boot out to touch Grenniger just to make certain he was still there. Or perhaps he just imagined doing this as well.

~

Sunlight came hard and sudden. Haish found himself awake, unconvinced that he had ever slept. They ate biscuits softened with a little canteen water, then stood and kept on up the trail.

They reached the top and started down the switchbacks. When the shrubs started, the fence appeared again. Haish wrote in his notebook: *Above treeline, fence cannot prosper.*

The wire changed: *hand-applied barbing, staple-barbs improvised from fencing staples. Barbs irregular, loose, on a single – rather than double – strand.*

There was a valley below, sign of habitation as well. They could see along the bottom of the valley a glistering river as winding as the path they were taking down the mountain. They kept walking, Haish with his notebook out, counting fence posts again, striking hashmarks, writing *A staple-barb is a barb not meant as a barb, a barb must be forced out of it*, pursing the paths of his own brain, letting his feet fall where they would.

III.

Wind cut through the stand of aspen. The scrunt of leaves and of the river lodged in Grenniger's ears. There was a pain in his chest. When he lifted his shirt, he discovered a dollar-sized bruise near his heart. He could not think how he came to have it.

He wiped the corners of his eyes, but when he looked at his fingers saw evidence of neither blood nor flux. The handkerchief across his face was stiff with sweat and dust. Getting up, he stamped his legs awake, then got a stick and prodded Haish awake as well.

"How do you feel?" he asked.

Haish stretched. "Not dead yet," he said. "And yourself?"

"Fine," lied Grenniger. "Get ready," he said.

Picking up the rifle, he scrambled down to the riverbank and out onto the rocks. He washed his face and filled his canteen, then stood drying his hand on his shirt.

He climbed up the bank, moving away from the camp to mount a slight rise. At the top he could glimpse through the trees a farmhouse. Leaning against a tree, he waited.

There was something amiss with Haish, an oddness that seemed rooted in the notebook which Haish now kept buttoned within his shirt, taking it out only to write in it, which he did now with greater and greater frequency. *Perhaps*, Grenniger thought, *Haish has been hired by the company not only to check fence but to observe me.* Haish's reluctance to pursue the contagion could be feigned, a way of getting him to lower his guard. Perhaps Haish was recording anything he judged to be a variation of procedure. Later, Grenniger would have to answer for everything.

There was no smoke from the chimney, no visible livestock. The barn doors were open, one of them swinging with the wind, the other's bottom edge grounded in the dirt.

I will threaten Haish with the rifle. I will hold the rifle on him and demand he surrender the notebook.

He felt Haish behind him, but did not turn, instead picking his way forward, toward the farm.

~

The barn was empty, nothing dead nor alive, though there were droppings and mouldered hay bales and other signs that livestock had been kept there recently. Haish was breathing behind him. Grenniger poked his rifle into the straw a few times then left for the farmhouse.

The door was unlocked. Inside, the place was close and dusty, cobwebs in the corners.

Four dishes were lined, one after another, along the centerline of a coarse and unvarnished pine table, the white wood smudged with the dark impressions of fingers. Beneath the table was a pair of men's boots with scuffed throats and worn-down heels. A slit-open sack of flour slouched on the counter, and when Grenniger reached his hand in, it came out white, except where it was speckled with tiny beetles. He shook them off.

"Anybody home?" he called.

Besides the sack of flour was a smallish tin box which, when Grenniger opened it, he found to be full of dried leaves. He set it down and a moment later Haish stuffed it into his saddlebags.

"We aren't about to hurt you," Grenniger shouted. "Come on out."

Haish was opening the bedroom door. Over Haish's shoulder, Grenniger could see a four-poster covered with a homemade quilt. In the middle of the quilt lay an airy and incongruent circle of lace. He pushed past, thrust the gun barrel under the bed, then fell to his knees and saw there was nothing there.

~

Half-rotted posts, top and middle strands of coldweather undulate wire, Grenniger read. Bottom strand: single-wire set with spur-wheels: large sheet metal, 14 sharpened points, locked in place with sheet metal tabs.

All the time I am eying Grenniger, trying to determine if he is afflicted. But the contagion only latterly gives up its traits and there is no means to foresee it. One has it or one does not, and once one knows one has it, one is already dead.

Are we already dead?

When Haish began to stir, Grenniger carefully slid the book back into the man's shirt.

~

A shoat, wedged between the bottom wire's spurred wheel and the ground, three bloody grooves carved into its back. It was half-standing, the spurs of the wheel deeply embedded. When they came closer, they realized it was still alive.

They stood beside the wire, watching. Grenniger prodded it with his boot and it squealed high.

"We observe," said Haish. "I quote. 'We don't meddle.'"

Ignoring him, Grenniger lifted the bottom wire. The spur pulled free from the shoat's back with a sound like crumpling paper, coming out bright at the bottom tips, a crust of blood rimming the brightness from above. The shoat tried to struggle to its feet, could not.

"Feed it," said Grenniger.

"I'm not about to waste my food on a dying piglet," said Haish.

"Come on," said Grenniger. "Help me."

Instead, Haish lifted his boot, brought its heel down hard against piglet's back. There was an underwater snap, more sensation than sound, and then the shoat lay quivering. Grenniger brought up the rifle, pointed it at Haish's chest.

"Since when did you have a fondness for swine?" asked Haish. "Besides," he said, pushing the animal over with the tip of his boot to reveal the blood dried into clumps on its underbelly, "where I come from, you don't feed a contagion, you starve it."

~

There was, they could see even from a distance, something on the fence perhaps a mile ahead. It became a scarecrow, and then, as they approached further, a man.

He was dead, fence-strung, the barbs hooked by design into his shirt and belt and keeping him afloat on the wire. His white shirt rippled with wind.

Careful not to touch the flesh, they sawed with knives at the cloth until the man sprawled off the wire to collapse in the dirt.

"We should have left him up," said Haish.

"Why?"

"What good does it do him to be lying on the ground?"

"What good does it do him to be strung on the fence?"

"At least he scared the birds away."

"What birds? There aren't any birds."

"Proof it was working."

Grenniger considered shooting Haish. Instead he prodded the corpse over.

The head rolled back and he saw the neck strung with oval bruises. He thought for an instant they were indications of fever.

"Almost refreshing to see a man merely strangled," Haish said.

There was something at the man's waist, a pouched apron which, when Haish slit the pouches open with his knife, proved to be full of short strands of wire and a barbing tool.

"Company man?" asked Haish.

"Don't think so," said Grenniger. "Not on this side of the border."

"We are on this side of the border."

"We're the exception."

"Perhaps we're not as exceptional as we'd care to believe."

"Perhaps not," said Grenniger. "But the company always sends them out in pairs."

But Haish, instead of listening, was prodding the man's bruised neck with his boot tip.

"You think we're in danger?" he asked.

"Yes," said Grenniger. "If we ever run into somebody alive."

~

The road became wider. At night, they slept in wheat fields beginning to run wild. At times they saw figures ahead, but before they could reach them, they vanished within the undulations of the road.

They passed a pair of horses in a dirt-caked corral, still standing but with blood spread all over their fronts. Haish began to speak of going back again. Grenniger told him he didn't care what he did as long as he shut up. While they argued, first one horse then the other pitched over.

They came across a section where the fence was down, post after post lying on the ground, chopped through, the barbed wire snipped to pieces.

"Fence cutters," said Haish.

"Write out a fine," said Grenniger.

"A fine?" said Haish. "We're on the wrong side of the border."

"Write it out anyway."

He wrote a fine for the fence, a deadline for repairs, then tore it out of his notebook. He left it fluttering on the first standing post, using a rock to drive a fencing staple through it.

In his notebook he wrote: *23 creosoted white-oak posts down, cut wire. Fine administered to unknown fence owner on Grenniger's recommendation, against the recommendation of this recorder.*

~

The fence broke into a simple three-prong barb. They passed an acreage scattered with the bodies of afflicted and lowing cattle, the same blood and lack of wound, the fence still intact.

Ahead Grenniger made out the glimmer of a town but said nothing. Later, near mid-afternoon, Haish saw it himself.

In the evening, darkness coming down, they debated whether they should move through the town or pass around it. Grenniger insisted they stick to the fence and, if the fence ended or turned sharply, continue in the direction the fence had last taken. Haish kept trying to protest, arguing for avoiding the town altogether.

They argued until they fell asleep. As soon as he awoke Grenniger started walking. Haish, as he had been doing all along, followed.

The town was little more than a single main street, a lone long block, the road running quickly through and out the other side.

The street was deserted. They stepped up onto the boardwalk, swung the doors of the saloon, saw it to be filled with several score of grim-faced men. The bar had been overturned, the broken glass of bottles scattered in sharp hooks along the floorboards. The men closest to them raised their hands.

"Mercy," said one of them. "We have no money. Mercy. We are good and faithful men."

"What?" said Haish. "We're not thieves," he said, and pulled his handkerchief off his face. Grenniger following his lead, lowered the gun. "Just checking fence."

A murmur went through the men. Grenniger could see now that behind the first row the others were holding pitchforks and hoes and wooden chairlegs with nails in them. He took a half-step backward toward the door.

"You say you follow the fence?"

Grenniger hesitated, nodded.

"Praise be!" said the man who had first spoke. "Praise be!" The rest were shouting as well, and flowing toward them and embracing them so vigorously and violently that if Grenniger had been able to get the gun up in the press, he wouldn't have hesitated to shoot. He had been without contact so long that the feel of their hands and arms, the smell of their breath coupled with the thought of contagion still heavy in his head, was too much to bear. Haish, shouting, was being carried away in the rush, and then all the doors of the town were thrown open, what seemed hundreds of people streaming out, the press of the crowd growing bigger all the while.

~

Later, when they were settled, the crowd subsided and gone, they were allowed to sup with the man who had broken the silence, a man named Glidden, in a room above the saloon. Glidden sat on the bed, legs crossed, Grenniger and Haish sitting in cane-back chairs, holding their hats. Three bowls of a watery stew were brought. Glidden looked into each then parceled them out.

"You say you follow the fence," said Glidden, once they had eaten. "Yet you do not believe."

"Believe what?" asked Haish.

"Yet you follow the fence."

"We've been hired," said Grenniger, "two dollars a day. Pursuit of the contagion along the fence to its end."

"Hired? By believers?"

"What do you mean, believers?" asked Haish.

"By the company," said Grenniger.

"The company," said Glidden. "They sent you to find me?"

"Are you the source of the contagion?" asked Grenniger. "Otherwise, no, they never said a word about you."

Glidden turned to Haish. "You have kept records," he said.

"What do you mean by 'records'?" Haish asked carefully.

"Meditations on the fence," said Glidden, "notes on its condition."

"Perhaps he has something of the kind," said Grenniger. "But they belong to the company."

"The company is benighted," said Glidden. "I have abandoned the company and gone into enterprise for myself. Return, tell them I shall not come back."

"But they didn't send us after you," said Haish.

"All they know can be fit into this single finger," said Glidden, lifting his thumb. "My friends," he said, "we are but a simple community, yet we are well on our way to perfection. We thirst for knowledge and guidance. If I am not mistaken, Mr. Haish, you belong among us. Give me your notebook, and then join with me."

"What about him?" asked Haish.

"Him?" said Glidden. "It is only by chance he is involved in this enterprise. He knows nothing of us. You, on the other hand, have been led to us."

He held out his hand. Haish reached into his shirt, and Grenniger could see the outlines of his knuckles against the cloth as he took hold of the book. "Let me think, let me think," said Haish, his voice oddly strangled. Grenniger cocked his rifle, pointed it at Glidden's head.

"You don't want to kill a man, Mr. Grenniger. Surely the company would object to that."

"I don't think the company would much mind."

"But over such a trifle, Mr. Grenniger?"

"The notebook belongs to the company," said Grenniger.

"The company deserves neither this book nor this man," said Glidden calmly. "The company has abandoned you."

"Haish?" said Grenniger. "What would you have me do?"

Yet suddenly Haish, his eyes gone hazy, seemed to have lost the will to respond.

Standing, Glidden walked to Haish's chair. He unfastened two buttons of Haish's shirt, reached in to pull out the notebook. Opening it, he began to read. "*Spur-wheels: large, sheet metal, 14 point, sharpened wheel locked in place with metal tabs.* Each spur-wheel an eternal round, Mr. Haish," he expounded, the book slapping shut. "Food for thought. Perpendicular to this, the running wire, fence-post to fence-post. One might think of each fence-post as a year, the wire as the course of a life. Each life is encircled, protected again and again by eternity in the form of the spurred wheel."

"What do you know about the contagion?" Grenniger asked.

"The contagion? Mr. Grenniger, there is no contagion. What you think of as contagion is merely an extension of wire, for not all wire is physical. This contagion is no more than animals bound in a wire too fine for their vision to perceive."

Returning to the bed, he opened the book, reading to himself as Haish sat motionless. Grenniger kept his finger on the trigger of the rifle. "You have done well," Glidden finally said to Haish. "But there is still much to learn. You shall know the fence and the fence shall make you free."

Haish said nothing.

Glidden nodded to Grenniger. "You can see your friend shall remain with us," he said. "If you choose to impede him, you will be killed. You are free to go."

IV.

Notebook returned, he was assigned a room above the saloon, told to continue to write. Glidden visited him twice daily: once in the late morning, once in the evening. He would take the notebook, examine what had been written, either correct it or expound upon it, use it as an occasion for instruction. *You are but an instrument,* Glidden sometimes said, and, of the notebook, *this work shall be one of the chief posts from which the wire is strung.*

Haish wondered about the company, whether they would send others after him as he and Grenniger had been sent after Glidden – if they had, in fact, been sent after Glidden. He did not think so, yet Glidden kept insisting. He did not write of this in the book. He thought himself canny and careful about what he included, though there were moments when his thoughts were so full with what he knew did not belong in the notebook that he could not write and even shook while holding the pencil. He did not know why he was there nor why he did not seem to have power to leave. At such moments Glidden stayed with him longer, stroked his forearms, whispered to him words of encouragement. He was filled at once with resentment and gratitude. *The paper is an untrammeled space,* Glidden would suggest. *Words must serve in the stead of a fence.* For a few days Haish would struggle and then, suddenly, begin to write again.

"Excellent," Glidden said, marking the notebook with his thumb. "Everything shall be as wire."

Mostly Haish felt befuddled, hardly knew what Glidden was talking about. He could not understand what he could write that would possibly be of value, but there Glidden was, reading and nodding, reading and expounding, as if the notebook itself had provoked the behavior. Haish tried to get up and leave the room but Glidden pressed firmly on his shoulders, forcing him down to the bed again. Then Glidden was gone and Haish got up again but found the door locked, the window nailed closed.

They were putting something in the food, something that confused him, he was certain of it, almost certain. It was not impossible at least. Yet there was no other food and if he did not eat the meal himself, Glidden would appear and force it down his throat. There was no place to hide the food, no place to dispose of it.

~

He finished eating then stumbled his way out of bed. For a change, the door was ajar. He was out into the hall, saw a corridor of small doors, at the end of the hall a staircase leading down.

He fumbled at the doors. He opened one, saw beyond it a room similar to his own, a man in a bed. He looked for a notebook, saw none.

He tried the next door, saw a similar tableau, a man in a bed, drowsy-eyed and barely able to look at him. He wondered briefly what his own eyes looked like. This time he did see a notebook lying in the man's lap, a pencil half lost in the blankets beside him.

He opened all the doors and left them ajar, made his way carefully down the stairs.

The saloon was deserted. Pushing his way through the swinging doors, he staggered along the boardwalk half-blinded by the sun. Then there were hands upon him and he found himself being taken, redirected, led back upstairs to his room.

"What of the others?" he asked Glidden.

"What others?" said Glidden. "You're the only one."

He was not the only one, he knew, but he seemed less and less certain of it with each moment. He focused on what was before his eyes. There was the room and the pencil, a hand holding the pencil that he deduced was his own. The book was only slowly filling up. The desire came to him to leave, but the door seemed never again to be unlocked.

There came then a period of great confusion where he could not even hold the pencil and found himself looking at everything as if it (or perhaps he himself) were lodged in the bottom of a hole. Glidden was there, encouraging him, regarding him strangely, telling him that this was his trial. He could hardly make out Glidden's individual words, deriving sense from them only after lengthy delay. They brought him a device and put it in his hands and he thought it some sort of interpretive tool. He folded it into his fist. He sensed Glidden's voice as a dull humming in his head and felt what little willpower he had left slowly strained away.

They opened the door and left it open. He did not move toward it. Instead, he found it preferable to remain where he was.

~

Slowly, almost imperceptibly, the hole began to be filled in, objects rising to the surface. Still he did not want to stand and attempt to breach the door. Instead he preferred to remain where he was. The pencil was still in his hand and he realized that the device that had been placed in his other hand was a tool for crimping barbs onto wire. It was a common object, nothing special about it, he told himself, yet somehow he could not make himself believe it: it was as if the tool had brought him back to consciousness.

He wrote of this in the notebook. When Glidden read it, he nodded.

"I want to show you something," he said.

Glidden took him by the hand and led him out of the room and down the stairs. They came into the empty saloon and then out on the boardwalk and then crossed the dirt street to the other boardwalk. They were at the door to a large building, a large barn or warehouse of some kind, and Glidden had dragged out a ring of keys and was opening the door.

Inside were scattered waist-high spools of bare wire, a bucket of fencing staples, a careful pile of fenceposts, several buckets of coarse salt. On the floor were rows of hand-crimpers and jointers and barb-spanners. There was an angled, double-handled dull blade he knew was for debarking a fencepost. There was an externally-geared, chain-cranked apparatus that looked like a boiler lying on its side. He did not know what to make of it.

The walls were run with strands of barbed-wire of all types and all varieties, an elaborate armature for the room. To see so much wire together rather than sparsed out along miles of fence made Haish's head purl. There was sheet metal spur, cast spool with inserted wire spur, two-point block-and-nail barb, serrated rail, three-point sheet-metal barb, two- three- and four-point wire barb of all coilage, splint barb, nail barb, knife-edged t-bar, edge-drilled warning block and side-drilled warning block, warning plate and warning ball, knife-edge grooved rail, tack ribbon, double tack, solid and hollow cockleburs, slit wire barbing, staple barbs, one-point loopings, swingers, spreaders, open diamond point, pitted point, closed diamond point, taper barb, single-wrap, double-wrap, hangers, wide-wrap, twist and cut, cut and span, long-wrap, winding, caduceus, spiral, prong, kink, kink and coil, kink and wrap, hitch and loop, loop and fastener, loop lock, washer-lock, ring-lock, clip-on, hitch, half-hitch, cross stick, saddle, nail lock, necktie, spanner, Australian kink, clasp, open-spanner, bend, simple-bend, double-z, triple tie, twins, spool and spur, horn-barb, six-point, eight-point, flat hook, peavy hook, thorn, tattered leaf, blunt-point, notched plate, butt plate, sleeve and strap, clip, spread and half-spread, grooved-diamond, wedged, single-plate, kink and shield, kink and star, swinging plate, spindled, pivot, arrow point, three-point short, key-lock, rider, socket, collared star, anvil, grooved pin, horn, stinger, curb, choked-burr, spinner, spur wheel, swaged-spur, joined saucer, concertina, wrap and wraparound, barb and lap, strip and tack, disc, perfect and needle-point, ribbed, spear-point, cleat, rowel, screw, center-core, spring, cactus-point, outside coil, conductor, rotating-coil, hook and point lock, gull wing, ladder, crossover, dropped loop, body grip, pigtail, snake tongue, knee grip, offset, seated, webbed, caged, trapped.

~

When his pencil blunted or lost its tip sometimes he went on writing, scratching invisible lines page by page until Glidden came and provided him a new pencil, turned the pages back. When he reached the last page, he filled the inside back cover. He went on to the outside back and then the inside front. When he reached, on the first page, words, he hesitated, then began to blot up the margin.

In time they took the notebook away. He waited, pencil in hand, for Glidden to bring him another. When nothing came, he began on the walls, pursuing a running line around them.

Glidden was with him much of the time, squinting his eyes and reading the wall. At least it felt as if Glidden were there. Haish would talk to Glidden, to Grenniger too. He was to finish writing, he told Grenniger, then he would be ready to pursue the fenceline, just a minute, just a minute. When he turned Grenniger was never there. He could not figure where Grenniger had gone. Grenniger would not go anywhere without him, would he? It had to be that Grenniger was sitting in the chair behind him, and when he turned to look at him he was simply elsewhere in the room. If he spoke, surely Grenniger could hear him.

Glidden was there, holding the notebook that had been taken from him, telling Haish that he had opened new pathways, yet when he looked about the room there was only the single door still and no pathway of any kind, unless it was his bare, horned feet, beating a pathway into the floorboards as they shuffled around the perimeter of the room.

Glidden was expounding upon a doctrine that remained unclear to Haish. Haish had suddenly the feeling that something had spun amiss. Glidden was gesturing to the walls, the words covering them. "I am concerned you do not restrict yourself to a notebook."

"Grenniger?" said Haish.

"Excuse me?" said Glidden.

Haish repeated the name, less emphatically now, but Glidden seemed not to respond. Haish began to stumble about the room, hand trailing on the wall, crying his friend's name. Then Glidden had him and was holding him still, stroking the back of his head. It felt so pleasant that Haish could not think what he had been doing a moment earlier.

V.

He had been walking for hours, following fence, still thinking of Haish and the notebook. The bruise on his chest spread until it wrapped one side of his torso, but there seemed, other than that, no sign of contagion. The pain was only slight.

In the morning he passed a body in the road, hat covering its face, shirt damp with blood. He circled it wide, continued forward. There were, a little farther, fresh ashes and more broken fence. He equated the one with the other, felt that he was in close pursuit now of fence cutters. If he found them, he was not sure whether he would join them or kill them.

The fences that remained standing were not machine-made but only splint barbs on single-strand wire, barbs stabilized with wire wrapping.

The road came to a crossroads and he continued forward, though that road was slighter than the others and drew close to the river. It became little more than a path, largely overgrown with grasses. The fence running beside it he could hardly see. He had to keep stepping off the road and prodding vegetation aside to see the thin, greased wire armed with splint-barbs.

He was walking on and off the road when it took a curve and he came upon the fence-cutters. There were three, faces covered with handkerchiefs tucked up into their hats, holes cut for eyes. One held a pair of large-handled wire cutters, the second held the wire taut. The last, standing idle, seemed to be directing the operation. When they glimpsed him and his rifle, they froze.

"Walk on past, Mister," the idle one, apparently the leader, said. "You don't know what you walked into."

"What do you have against fence?" Grenniger asked.

All three of them looked at each other. "We got plenty against it," one wearing black boots said.

"You with Glidden?" asked Leader.

He shook his head.

"You from the company?" asked Black Boots.

Grenniger nodded.

They all three of them cursed. "You're on the wrong side of the border," Leader said. "They don't have no say in what goes on over here."

"You have guns," said Grenniger, then gestured at Black Boots. "Throw them down, one by one, starting with you."

They took their guns out, dropped them into the dirt, Leader holding onto his for a second too long so that Grenniger felt obliged to fire a shot over his shoulder. He made them move back and put their hands all on a post, then gathered their guns, the cutters.

"I should give you a fine," he said. "Should even kill you. But I'm in no mood, and besides, don't have the finebook."

"Fence don't belong here," said Leader.

"I don't disagree with you," said Grenniger, pocketing their guns. "But I have no interest in discussing questions of belief. If you know what's good for you, you won't follow me."

~

He continued on his way, struggling awkwardly under the bulk of the cutters, guns, saddlebag. He watched the fence cutters keep hold of the post until he was over the rise and down. He hurried forward.

He threw the cutters out in the field where they couldn't be seen from the road, but kept the guns. At dark, he kept walking for a time, then left the road and twisted between the strands of wire, went out into the field.

He threw down his saddlebags then lay down himself. Taking his knife out of the sheath, he hid it under the saddlebags and slept with the rifle across his knees.

All night he dreamt of figures moving through the grass toward him and the report of the rifle in his hands as he killed them. When he awoke, he was not surprised to see the three of them there, still masked, the rifle just being jerked off his knees and out of his hands. The rifle went off and kicked backward. Before him, a man's knee shattered and spat blood and he saw the man in black boots collapse, shrieking. He realized he still had hold of the rifle with one hand, then other hands were back on the barrel and stock. He felt his forefinger break against the trigger and thought if they kept pulling he might lose the rifle altogether, his finger too, then the weapon was out of his hands, the finger stripped of flesh along one side and turned crooked and already darkening about the joint.

Cutters had the rifle and was pointing it at Grenniger's face, smiling furiously in a way that showed his teeth.

"I told you to walk on," Cutters said. "I damn told you."

The other man stood over Black Boots, who continued to scream, grabbing his leg. Cutters pulled the rifle's trigger. Nothing happened. He had begun to work the action, cocking the gun, but Grenniger's good hand already had hold of the knife under the saddlebags. He turned and stood and swung in the same motion and Cutters shrugged his shoulders up to block the blow. His arms were meant to come up too but he would not let go of the rifle. The knife pierced his throat, the knife's barb tearing his windpipe open and he was falling, wheezing, until Grenniger had the rifle in his own hands again.

"Hands up," he said, and imagined for a bare instant he was still wearing the handkerchief over his face.

They put their hands up, except Cutters who was occupied wheezing and trying not to choke on blood, and Black Boots who was busy grabbing his leg.

"I asked you not to follow me," Grenniger said. He walked over to the man with the shot-out knee. The leg hung askew.

"Take off his boots," he said to the still-healthy man. "Then take off your slit-throat friend's, then remove your own." Black Boots screamed as his leg was moved.

~

He carried the triune of paired boots for a while then threw them, singly, as far into the weeds as he could muster. His stripped thumb ached and swelled. In the end he wrapped it in his handkerchief, tying it off and leaving the ends of the cloth hanging down in awkward wings.

From time to time he looked behind him, but there seemed no pursuit. After a while he slept. When he awoke he unwrapped his thumb and stared at it, found it to have turned black during the night. His whole body was sore and he did not dare look under his shirt. *I will turn back*, he told himself. He continued on.

He entered into older fence, the wire strung with horseshoe nails bent around into single-point barbs. The land was rocky and scrappy, yet he could see, at some little distance, horses alive and grazing. There was too, on the side of the road, the body of a man, the hands knotted in fists, a floppy-brimmed hat tightened over its face. He plucked the hat off, expecting to find empty sockets and grinning teeth, and was shocked to find instead a chunk of wood, the head missing entirely.

By mid-day he was in foothills. The fence ended and he wondered if he had concluded his arrangement with the company. *pursue contagion along fenceline stop.* How was one to read *stop*? How was he to determine when he could stop?

~

His eyes were stinging. He reached up and rubbed first one then the other with the back of his hand. When he pulled his hand away he thought he saw thin pale red strokes.

He felt slightly disoriented. He kept climbing, leaving the path without noticing, slipping into a dry streambed, plodding carefully along smoothed rocks until the bed split into smaller flows, disappeared entirely.

He stumbled on through aspen, the leaves fluttering with wind. He could feel blood push in his ears as he came up against a rocky slope and began to pull himself up it. The rock was sharp and his fingers began to bleed and his chest was bleeding now too but he kept climbing.

The face leveled out to a gentle slope. He found himself standing on the top of a ridge, looking down to the other side.

He beheld a vast and fenceless and barren plain, unbounded and running on forever.

There was no source to the contagion, he realized. It was simple and endless.

He began his descent.

VI.

There was no source to the contagion, he realized, Haish wrote. *It was simple and endless.*

He gathered his breath. There were moments which seemed to have been wiped away, when he was writing on the wall and then suddenly would find himself in a bed. Or he would begin to read from the point where his writing had changed – *He had been walking for hours, following fence, still thinking of* – until he had circled the walls enough to grow dizzy and confused.

~

He opened his eyes to see Glidden there, reading the walls around, shaking his head, then shaking him.

"This is not what you believe," Glidden said. "Not this at all."

Haish, confused, tried to figure in his head what *this* might refer to.

"You must not think of Mr. Grenniger," said Glidden. "You must think of wire."

"Grenniger?" asked Haish.

"Mr. Grenniger, I assure you, is healthy and robust, returned already to the company. He is not contagioned nor wandering in some waste, for neither waste nor contagion exist. All you ascribe to him has not occured."

Haish looked about for Grenniger, could not seem to see him. He was nervous and uncomfortable, the inside of his mouth dry.

"Where is Grenniger?" he asked.

"Such promise," said Glidden. "You must refuse to surrender to doubt, for doubt leads quickly to heresy."

But Haish was up and stumbling about the room, calling Grenniger's name, searching the walls, touching Grenniger's name wherever it appeared.

~

Glidden was beside him, coaxing him up. He rose and was surprised by how distant his legs felt. Glidden had his arm and suddenly he was through the door. He slipped on the stairs, but Glidden propped him up. They were in the sunlight and he felt the boardwalk momentarily under his feet, and then felt the dirt, then boardwalk again. They were inside and he was being led forward, past wire-strung walls. His wrists were manacled against one another and attached to a chain, the other end of the chain around a ring in the ceiling, above his reach.

He was left alone. When he tried to sit, he felt his arms tighten against the chain. He could rest on his knees, but it kept his arms stretched and taut. He kept standing up and trying to sit, standing, trying to sit.

There was no food and nothing brought to him. He slept in flashes on his feet or on his knees. He went for a time without food, yet somehow his head seemed to be clearer. His arms ached, as did his knees. The edge of the manacles had begun to gouge away the flesh at his wrists.

~

Faintly but finally lucid, he saw Glidden standing before him, behind him a wash of pale faces.

"How do you feel?" Glidden asked.

He didn't bother to answer.

"You have become bound up," said Glidden, touching his chest.

He looked down at his own chest, saw that blood had started to seep through his shirt. He looked up and saw that Glidden had parted his own shirt, revealing underneath a webwork of scars. Behind him he could see a field of bared chests, the same awful webwork replicated.

"There is the physical wire and the spiritual wire," said Glidden. "The body knows to heal from the one but it must be coaxed to recognize the other. We must fight wire with wire."

They were at the walls, taking the barbed strips into their own hands. They were all about him and he felt pain as he breathed and understood they were wrapping wire tight around his chest until it pierced his skin.

The blood began to come more readily instead of merely seeping. He could feel above the pain in his arms and wrists and knees a sharp pricking each time he breathed.

He breathed in, out, in, out, the pricking growing duller, and fading into the rhythm of his breathing, becoming almost comfortable, until he began to believe he could go on like that forever.

When the pain was at an ebb, he began to sense the structure of the contagion itself, the hidden system of post and wire. He pursed his mouth as if listening. *Two strand wire*, it seemed to be. He needed his notebook and pencil to record it. Just knowing he needed them made him feel almost as if he had them. That was it:

Post: flesh and bone.

Pain distant, wire around his chest a mere pressure now. It was only this pressure, curiously in his skull rather than on the surface of his body, that informed him that he continued to breathe. *Two-strand wire, improperly twisted and now largely separate, one wire tangible, the other not, held in proximity by—*

The pencil in his skull dropped, clattered away. The hand that had been holding it grew numb. What was left of him waited to see how long it would take for post to give way, fence to collapse.

Malcher in the Dark

I.

Malcher managed to free himself while his guard, drunk, dozed. He waited until he heard the sound of the man snoring, then wormed his way across the dirt to the tent wall, wriggling his way under the canvas and out into the open air. Not far away, he could hear the other three men talking around the fire. They were drunk too, talking a little too loudly, happy over having caught him and already spending the reward money in their heads. If they hadn't been so loud, they probably would have heard him.

He worked his way to a fallen tree, propped himself against it and, grunting, managed to climb to his feet. He could see the men now, outlined by the flames, blotting portions of the fire out. His hands were still tied behind his back, but it would be a mistake to stay long enough to work them free. Better to get as far away as possible as quickly as he could. They'd change shifts soon and another man would take over as guard, and that would be that. How much time did he have? It couldn't be long.

He began to walk, hunched a little, keeping on the balls of his feet and trying to make as little noise as possible. Whatever moonlight there was, was blotted out by the canopy above. At first the light cast by the fire was enough that it was simple to pick his way through the trees, but with each step it grew harder to see. Soon, if he'd had his hands free, he would have been waving them in front of him. As it was, he had to push forward until he ran into something, and then try to figure out – from what was touching his face or his legs or his chest – whether he could go through or had to go around. He moved too quickly, and the sharp tip of a dead branch tore open his face. He stumbled back, ignoring the stinging of his cheek, and chose another way forward.

A few steps later, his foot caught on something and he fell, sprawling. Had the men around the fire heard? He held his breath until finally he heard their voices pick up again, a low murmur in the distance. He breathed out, relaxed.

Feeling about for something to use to pull himself upright, he found what he had tripped on: a jag of stone jutting just above the duff. He turned his back to it so he could feel it with his fingers. The edge was not sharp exactly, but was at least rough. Sidling backward, Malcher positioned his hands so that the rope around his wrists was crossing this coarse edge, then began to saw back and forth.

It was awkward. Quickly his arms grew tried, his neck tightening, his hands tingling and growing numb. Was it working? Since his hands were tied behind his back, he had little way to tell. He could only hope it was – he couldn't think what else to do. He kept sawing, back and forth, back and forth, sometimes slipping and abrading his wrists or hands.

~

He wasn't sure how much time had passed. Five minutes at least, maybe quite a bit longer. He kept sawing, sawing. It had to be working, had to.

He heard a distant shout, and then several raised voices. Words too mangled by distance for him to make out exactly what was being said, but he could guess. He sawed faster. Suddenly things began to loosen.

Then came the sound of someone crashing through the undergrowth. Halloos passing back and forth between the men.

"Malcher!" called a voice, altogether too close for comfort. It was Byrne. "You bastard, where in hell you got to?"

He didn't answer. Of course he didn't. The rope had frayed just enough for him to work his hands loose. He chafed his wrists.

"Malcher, come on out!"

Slowly he rolled into a crouch. Was it the right moment to run?

Not yet.

He could see the glow of the guttering brand Byrne had dragged from the fire. The man was still a little way away, probably fifteen or twenty yards. The brand didn't cast much light. Maybe Byrne would walk in the other direction without discovering him.

But Byrne just stayed there, thrusting the brand in one direction and then another, peering in a circle all around him. Malcher was still shy of its glow, but just barely.

"Malcher!" Byrne called again. "Come out now and all will be forgotten! We'd rather turn you in alive than dead."

Something crashed through the undergrowth near Byrne. One of the others drawing closer. Byrne swung his brand toward the noise. As soon as he did, Malcher leapt up and started running full bore.

From behind, Byrne cried out and the other man, whichever he was, did too. Malcher kept running. Hands outstretched, he tried to keep the branches away from his face. He kept striking things, crashing into them. He was, he realized, leaving a trail that, with their torches, they would have no trouble following, but he didn't know what else to do but keep running.

A shot rang out, passing close enough for him to hear the bullet's whine. The ground suddenly dipped below his feet and he stumbled, falling onto a level floor of rounded rocks – a dry creek bed, he realized. His knee flared with pain. He scrambled up and limped down the path formed by the bed, his boots clacking and skittering over the rocks. This way at least he wouldn't run into any trees.

His boots were making too much noise: they heard and followed. He could see three lights now, behind and just above him, in pursuit. And then abruptly he reached the edge of the forest. Here there was starglow and a sliver of moon. There, a little distance away, that starless darkness was what must be the looming cliff face they'd rode past while it was still day. There had been a cave there – he remembered seeing the opening – and he rushed across the open ground, slipping and sliding, toward it.

They were close behind him now. They could see him better out here in the open. He heard two shots, one whining past nearby, the other going wild.

"Malcher!" shouted Byrne from behind. "Hold still and die!"

He didn't hold still. Another shot, and he felt a burst of pain in his tricep. He cried out involuntarily, nearly went down, but managed to stay upright, and then he had reached the cave and darted in.

II.

He tried to gather his breath. The cave smelled dry and dusty and he wasn't sure how deep it was. If it was shallow, a little declivity in the rock, then he was as good as dead. If it was even a little deeper, he might have a chance. *I have*, he lied to himself, *been in worse scrapes before.*

He pushed his way in, arms outstretched. Soon he encountered a side wall, and followed it along with his fingertips. Then his other hand touched the other wall on the other side. Slowly the walls came closer together. He kept expecting to reach the back of the cave, but he didn't. Even after a few dozen steps, there was still what seemed to be a purposeful tunnel curving back into the darkness.

Good, he thought.

He felt his way down the tunnel until he was sure he'd be out of sight of the cave's mouth and then stopped, waited.

He could hear the men clustering near the mouth of the cave, but so far they hadn't come in.

"Come on out!" one of them bawled. Not Byrne. Hopkins, maybe.

He didn't come out. He didn't bother to answer.

"Don't make us come in after you!"

When he saw the light from their torches growing on the curve of the tunnel wall, he shouted, "Not another step!"

"What you going to do?" said Byrne, voice thick with contempt. "Throw rocks?"

"I'm going to shoot you," said Malcher.

Byrne laughed. "With what?"

"With my gun."

"Like hell."

"Swear on my mother's eternal soul," lied Malcher. "A derringer. Model 95 double."

Byrne laughed again, but it sounded a little less confident this time. "Now how would you have stopped us from finding it all this time? Kept it up your arse?"

"Trick boot heel," said Malcher.

"There's not enough space for a goddamn derringer in a fucking boot heel. You're lying."

"Well then, come and get me."

Byrne didn't say anything. Malcher waited. In the silence he could hear a slow *drip, drip, drip*. He couldn't place what it was – water from the cave's ceiling, maybe – and then realized no, it wasn't that at all: it was blood dripping from the wound in his arm.

I should patch that up, he thought.

"If you've got a derringer, why didn't you use it already?"

"It's a two-shot, remember? Got to make both shots count."

"I don't believe you got nothing of the kind."

"You have two men to spare," said Malcher again. "Send them in."

Byrne didn't. Malcher could hear him whispering to one of the other men just shy of the cave's mouth. Then that man raised his voice. "Like hell I will!" he said.

"Now, now," said Byrne. "No need to get riled."

Then they were whispering again. Malcher waited, impatient. When the whispering stopped, he waited some more. Still nothing.

"Coming in or not?" he finally asked.

"We're coming in, all right,' said Byrne. "First thing in the morning. Once it's light and we can see to kill you."

He thought it through, there in the dark, waiting for morning. What were his options?

He could come out with hands raised and let them take him. With the right judge, maybe he'd get a dozen years or so. Depended on what they knew he'd done. Wrong judge, or they knew too much, he'd hang.

He could try to sneak out, past Byrne and his men, but they'd be ready for him now. He wouldn't make it past, and they'd likely kill him for trying.

He could push his way deeper into the cave, hope the tunnel led somewhere, to another exit. Or at least that it branched and forked enough that once they did come in he might be able to evade them.

Drip, drip, drip. He was still hearing it. How could he still be bleeding? He took out his handkerchief and tied it around his wounded arm. There.

But he could still hear the dripping. It was coming from closer to the mouth of the tunnel. It wasn't coming from his wound after all.

Feeling his way forward, he started down the tunnel.

~

It was very dark. He couldn't see a thing. At first his eyes strained to make something out and he found he was hallucinating little flashes of light, as if his optic nerves were shorting out. He closed his eyes, kept them closed.

He felt his way along. The tunnel curved as it went, gently, and seemed to slope downward just a little. It remained more or less the same size. Was it an old mine shaft? But no, there were no timber supports – none that his fingers brushed past anyway. Perhaps it was a natural tunnel. But wasn't it too regular for that?

There were no branchings. Just a single tunnel going deeper and down, curving deep into the mountain. Perhaps it would lead him through the mountain, to another way out. If it didn't, if it dead-ended without branching, they'd have no difficulty finding him come morning.

Abruptly he stopped. He was still hearing it, that same *drip, drip, drip*, always just behind him, as if the sound was pushing at his back, prodding him on.

No, he told himself, *that's impossible*. He must be imagining it. Or hearing some strangely distorted echo. A drip couldn't follow you.

"Hello?" he called. The word vanished as soon as it was said, as if swallowed. Not an echo then. And what was that smell, sharp and metallic?

He hesitated, feeling the darkness heavy around him. He held his breath, listened for the drip to come again. Nothing, no sound. He had imagined it: nothing to worry—

Drip.

Where was it coming from? Why was it always behind him? The smell, it suddenly came to him, was blood. He brought his wounded arm closer to his face and sniffed. Yes, that was the smell – but even if he held his arm very close indeed the smell was fainter than if he simply breathed in the open air.

He suddenly felt strange. It was all he could do not to flee back the way he had come. *But if you run*, a part of himself thought, *whatever it is will come after you.*

~

He waited, trying to bring his breathing under control. His fingers were shaking; he could feel them shaking even if he couldn't see them. He turned slowly around and began to walk back up the tunnel the way he had come.

Or at least he would have if there had not been, when he turned around, something in his path. At first he thought he had not turned around far enough and was running into one of the tunnel walls, but no, when he reached out, the walls were still there to either side. He tried to sidle around the barrier and it moved as he moved. When he reached out his hand to push it aside, something caught him by the wrist and held on. Tightly but carefully: it didn't hurt, but it was also quickly clear he'd be unable to shake himself free. He stood there, unable to go forward, unable to go back, unsure what to do.

Whatever it was slid closer.

"Hello," it whispered. Even though his own voice hadn't echoed when he called out, this whisper did, resounding back and forth all around him.

He blacked out.

III.

When he awoke, he was flat on the stone floor. His head ached. When he tried to bring his hand to his face, he found that something still had hold of his wrist.

"Hello," the voice whispered again.

He managed not to faint this time. He made a sound, a murmur that was equal parts fear and acknowledgment.

"I don't often have visitors," whispered the voice.

"No?" said Malcher, his voice cracking.

"Do you know why?"

"I can guess," said Malcher before he could stop himself.

"Oh?" said the voice. "What's your guess?" But Malcher said nothing, unsure that it would be wise to respond.

"Your hands are shaking," said the voice. "Your fingers too. I can feel them."

"I'm frightened," Malcher admitted.

The voice emitted a laugh that was like the slow crumpling of a piece of paper. "Of course you are," it said.

"What are you going to do with me?"

"All in good time," said the voice. Each time the voice spoke, Malcher tried to imagine a face and body to go along with it, but whatever image he thought up felt off, wrong. He wasn't even sure that what was holding his wrist was, technically, a hand. It mostly felt like a hand, except when it didn't.

"Those others," the voice whispered. "Will they come in after you?"

"Yes," said Malcher. "In the morning."

"Excellent," said the voice.

They remained in silence in the dark, Malcher at every instant aware of the appendage that might or might not be a hand encircling his wrist. Then he began to hear it again:

Drip.

Drip.

Drip.

"Is that coming from you?" Malcher asked.

"Hmm?" said the voice. "Oh that. Yes. From the grin in my throat."

The grin in its throat? wondered Malcher. But he didn't ask the question aloud: he didn't want to hear any more about it.

"That's why I whisper, too," said the voice. "Because of the slash."

"How long has it been dripping?" Malcher managed.

"Would it make you feel better if I told you?"

Malcher said nothing.

"Rhetorical question," said the voice. "We both know it wouldn't."

Again, Malcher fainted.

~

When he regained consciousness, his other wrist was being held as well. When he moved his arms, the voice's hands, if they were hands, moved along with them. He felt like he was a marionette.

"I'll make you a deal," whispered the voice.

Malcher whimpered.

"The men hunting for you, you coax them in here, you get them to come, far back, and I'll save you for last. If they're big enough, maybe I won't even bother with you. Maybe I'll feel full and generous and will let you go." The voice slid closer, was right beside his face now. "Are they big? Meaty?"

When Malcher tried to speak, nothing came out.

"There," whispered the voice. "You see? Things might be looking up for you."

He heard a shifting in the darkness in front of him, then the dripping resumed. The floor beneath him, he realized, was growing wet.

When the voice resumed, it had drifted further away. It seemed almost to be talking to itself now. "I'll just pick the one that's best, that's strongest. That one I'll save and use as a home." The voice gave a dry, crackling laugh. Somehow, despite the darkness, Malcher could feel the creature's face turning toward him. He imagined its eyes glittering. "You're not the strongest, are you?"

~

He did not know how much time had passed. An eternity maybe. At one point he felt the creature near his wounded arm, and then heard a gentle lapping. For a moment the arm stung, and then it quickly grew numb.

"Just a little something to keep up our spirits," whispered the voice. "Nothing to be concerned about."

More time passed, then even more. For long moments, Malcher could pretend that he was alone, and then he'd move a little and feel the grip around his wrists, or he'd hear the dripping again.

Finally, he began to hear the clatter of footsteps. They grew louder. It must, he realized, be morning.

"Malcher!" shouted Byrne. There was no echo to his voice either. Only the creature's voice echoed. "We're coming for you!"

"That's your cue," whispered the voice.

Malcher swallowed. He started to speak, but all that came out was a groan. He coughed and swallowed, and then tried again.

"Don't shoot!" he called. "I surrender!"

"A sensible decision. Come on out then," said Byrne. His voice was closer. The tunnel had started to lighten from the glow of Byrne's torch.

"I can't! I'm stuck. I need your help."

"Hands up, then," said Byrne, "and keep them up."

Malcher raised his hands high above his head. He looked down the tunnel toward where Byrne's voice was coming from. He was starting to be able to see. Soon he'd be able to see everything.

He stared down the tunnel, careful not to turn his head and look at whatever was there beside him. As long as he looked straight ahead, he told himself, there was at least a chance he would still survive.

Also by Brian Evenson:

Novels
Father of Lies (Four Walls Eight Windows, 1998; reprinted Coffee House Press, 2016)
Dark Property: An Affliction (Black Square Editions, 2002)
The Open Curtain (Coffee House Press, 2006)
Aliens: No Exit (Dark Horse Books, 2008)
Last Days (Underland Press, 2009)
Martyr (Tor, 2010)
Immobility (Tor, 2012)
Catalyst (Tor, 2012)
The Lords of Salem (with Rob Zombie) (Grand Central Publishing, 2013)
The Deaths of Henry King (with Jesse Ball) (Uncivilized Books, 2015)
Feral (with James DeMonaco) (Blumhouse Books, 2017)

Collections
The Din of Celestial Birds (Wordcraft of Oregon, 1997)
Contagion and Other Stories (Wordcraft of Oregon, 2000)
The Wavering Knife (Fiction Collective 2, 2004)
Fugue State (Coffee House Press, 2009)
Windeye (Coffee House Press, 2012)
A Collapse of Horses (Coffee House Press, 2016)
Song for the Unraveling of the World (Coffee House Press, 2019)
The Glassy, Burning Floor of Hell (Coffee House Press, 2021)

Now available and forthcoming from Black Shuck Shadows:

Shadows 1 – The Spirits of Christmas
by Paul Kane

Shadows 2 – Tales of New Mexico
by Joseph D'Lacey

Shadows 3 – Unquiet Waters
by Thana Niveau

Shadows 4 – The Life Cycle
by Paul Kane

Shadows 5 – The Death of Boys
by Gary Fry

Shadows 6 – Broken on the Inside
by Phil Sloman

Shadows 7 – The Martledge Variations
by Simon Kurt Unsworth

Shadows 8 – Singing Back the Dark
by Simon Bestwick

Shadows 9 – Winter Freits
by Andrew David Barker

Shadows 10 – The Dead
by Paul Kane

Shadows 11 – The Forest of Dead Children
by Andrew Hook

Shadows 12 – At Home in the Shadows
by Gary McMahon

Now available and forthcoming from Black Shuck Shadows:

Shadows 25 – Nine Ghosts
by Simon Bestwick

Shadows 26 – Hinterlands
by George Sandison

Shadows 27 – Beyond Glass
by Rachel Knightley

Shadows 28 – A Box Full of Darkness
by Simon Avery

Shadows 29 – That Fatal Shore
by Sean Hogan

Shadows 30 – The Flowering
by Alison Littlewood

Shadows 31 – Chasing Spirits
by John Llewellyn Probert

Shadows 32 – Black Bark
by Brian Evenson

blackshuckbooks.co.uk/shadows